Love and
Murder

Love and Murder

THE LAST VOYAGE OF THE EREWHON

BILL MOONEY

LOVE AND MURDER
THE LAST VOYAGE OF THE EREWHON

This is a work of fiction. All of the characters, names, incidents, organizations, and dialogue in this novel are either the products of the author's imagination or are used fictitiously.

iUniverse books may be ordered through booksellers or by contacting:

iUniverse LLC
1663 Liberty Drive
Bloomington, IN 47403
www.iuniverse.com
1-800-Authors (1-800-288-4677)

ISBN: 978-1-4917-4072-9 (sc)
ISBN: 978-1-4917-4074-3 (hc)
ISBN: 978-1-4917-4073-6 (e)

Library of Congress Control Number: 2014912493

Printed in the United States of America.

iUniverse rev. date: 08/12/2014

Prologue

When most people start out on a trip they pretty much know what lays ahead and what to expect only the truly adventurous would do otherwise. To say that Tommy and Val were up for *some* adventure would be true but there was another reason for making the trip in addition to the diving. They were in love but Val questioned if this was a love that would last, or was it just— *being in love*—rather than the deeper feeling for another, that was necessary for a lifetime together. The time on the ship would give them the opportunity to conclusively decide. Time away from studies, home and families would determine their future together, or even if there was to be a future together. There were other aspects of their lives to consider—this was decision time.

But events were to ensue that would change whatever fate previously awaited them, and in a way they could never have imagined. No matter what Tommy and Val's notions of the sea had been they could never have envisaged, nor could anything have prepared them for the macabre events that were to envelop them during their time on the Sailing Ship *Erehwon*.

One

Cape Upstart is situated close to the middle of the east coast of Australia about a thousand kilometers north of Brisbane. The sea almost surrounds a small hook of jutting land that allows sweeping views of coast and sea, that and the generally balmy climate make this little peninsular a particularly attractive spot. It is handsome places like Cape Upstart, and such towns as nearby Merinda, that make the Coral Sea Coast the unique place that it is. And of course, out there, beyond the breakers, the magnificence of the Great Barrier Reef itself.

A few of the divers had arrived and now waited on the dock for the launch that was, by this time, supposed to be there to take them out to the boat. Most of them showed the effects of long journeys from different places and although they were strangers to each other whatever inhibition there might be, soon melted. As more turned up they were easily recognized and greeted by those already there, as a brother or sister diver.

Tommy and Val sat on one of the wooden barriers on the wharf. They were first to get to the wharf and had introduced themselves as more arrived, among them several others from America, one a young man by the name of Spencer who Val figured could not be more that about sixteen. After the customary 'hi' and 'where you from?' exchange he moved away to re-join the rest of his group, a big athletic guy of twenty-something and others of about the same age all from the San Diego area. It was getting late in the day—the sun was still hot but most of them were shaded by tall trees growing right up to where the land ended and the dock began. There was also a cooling sea breeze that bought with it a strong scent of the ocean. Relaxed and patiently awaiting the launch, Val and Tommy talked quietly.

'And,' Val said emphatically, 'I don't want you backing out on the reason why we made this trip to Australia.'

'To have fun, relax and to see if it's really down under.' Val disregarded the quip.

'Yes, but the significant reason, is to give us the opportunity to find out if we should stay together or not, a subject that you are curiously adamantinely disinclined to discuss.'

'Sure, absolutely, we'll do that, Val,' he said breezily, 'but who in the hell says adamantinely?'

'Shrinks do. Tommy, you're not absolutely sure of anything,' Val gestured with her palms up and a shoulder shrug. 'On the plane down here to Australia you said you might even quit law.'

'I never said that, I said I didn't want to be my dad's office boy.'

'You wouldn't be his office boy, you'd be a lawyer.'

'A lawyer yes, but right now I'm only fifty-fifty on going into his firm. Mayhew Smith, Partners and Associates and since there's no Smith anymore it's dad's firm, Oliver Mayhew, Partners and Associates.' A fine point of law that Tommy could wrestle with could always capture his attention but the mundane day-to-day matters would bore him rigid. 'And as for the partners and associates,' he went on, 'they're a stuck up clique of law firm hacks, *and* I could be on the lowest rung for years.'

'Stop it! Tommy, Mayhew Smith is one of the most prestigious law firms in Philadelphia.'

'They're all crooks.' He persisted, trying to keep a straight face.

'They are not.' Val said dismissing it for the baseless wisecrack that it was.

'And so are most of the clients, crooks I tell you!' He alleged, faking solemnity, 'cheating on taxes and anything else they can get away with, believe me Val,' shaking his head and lowering his voice, 'it's a grubby business.'

'Oh, for God's sake will you please be serious? I'm going to enjoy you a lot more after you grow up, any idea when that's going to happen?'

'It's a slow process.'

'It sure is.'

'Okay, okay. So I get it done *and* pass the bar and baby, passing the bar is no slam-dunk —'

'Come on, you were in the top three per cent of your class!'

'Well,' Tommy said a little more seriously, 'so I pass, you know what? I think I'd like to do criminal law.'

'No you wouldn't.'

'Sure I would, I like desperadoes.'

Val sighed. 'You're odd.'

'Interesting little word, odd—and speaking of odd,' he said with a nod toward the others on the dock, 'have you taken a good look at our soon to be shipmates? Check them out. It's like someone called central casting and said send one of everything you got.'

'They're fine—just eclectic.'

'Only a clinical psychologist would say eclectic.'

'It's going to be another year before you can call me a psychologist.'

'So doctor is out?'

'For now, doctor is out.'

'But I can call you shrinko?'

'Certainly…. shyster.'

Thomas Mayhew and Valerie Castellano looked like they should be together, that they belonged together, the way some people do. Val with the light olive complexion that signposted her northern Italian ancestry—dark, lightly streaked hair—long but for now tied in a pony tail that poked out of the back of a well-worn New York Yankee's cap. Lovely dark eyes and an exquisitely shaped mouth that when she smiled, which was characteristic— and most of the time, displayed even, white teeth. And she had a body that any model would envy. Without doubt Val was nothing short of a knockout. Tommy, just a tad over average height with an even tan that seemed to be uninterrupted by the seasons and short brownish hair that tended to sun-bleach unevenly. His lineage descended from immigrants who had got themselves out of an impoverished and famine-ridden Ireland to America. Tommy was not especially handsome, he was rather, a well-set-up, overall good-looking guy.

Both were fairly athletic and from time to time, engaged in some form of outdoorsy things whenever their commitments allowed—they had dived before during a four day Florida vacation and liked it. They also looked like they came from relatively well-to-do families, which they did—but they didn't flaunt it. And neither of them cared about that anyway. They were clearly two people who would make their own way in the world.

Tommy was taking a year off before tackling the bar exams and to take a post-graduate course in Constitutional Statutes and, for no particular reason, some of the more uncommon aspects of International Law. And Val was in the final year of her clinical psychology degree. They had heard about the diving trip from another guest at one of those backpacker hotels on their third day in Australia. Tommy and Val knew it was something they had not even thought about but it seemed like a good deal, it cost pretty much nothing and all you had to do was some work on the boat, how hard could that be? And you got to dive the Great Barrier Reef. They bought the bare minimum of diving gear, flippers, face masks and so on—and said yes.

Tommy stood, stretched, took in a deep breath of the clean air and looked around. The sea, the town, to the other people on the dock. Then he sat back down and put his arm around Val's waist.

'About the . . . discussion, Val, can we just say: we'll see what we will see?'

'That's such a prosaicism.'

'And what the hell is that?'

'Prosaicism? . . . A cliché, a platitude.'

'Of course, we'll see what we will see, is a platitude.' Tommy retorted with a laugh, 'Every profession, 'every professional, has platitudes to get him off the hook from challenging questions—and they all mean nothing.'

'Give me a for instance?'

'Okay, for instance, a doctor will say "in the fullness of time"—a Priest or a Pastor will say "we are not meant to know everything" and a . . .'

Val cut in ... 'and a psychologist will say?'

'Hmmm . . . "well, what do *you* think about that?"'

'Smart-ass. And what do Lawyers say, platatudiously? "Justice must be seen to be done."'

'Naaaaa *and* platatudiously is not a word. Lawyers just keep saying—we'll see you in court, buddy!'

Val linked her arm in his and with a kiss on his cheek breathed, 'I'll say it again, my love—you're odd.'

The wheels of a bus grinding to a brake squawking halt near the dockside had them look back to the road. There were few people around and those that were showed only passing interest as Wally, Beth and Jim tumbled out exhibiting the fatigue due to a long bus trip. Like the earlier arrivals, they tossed their duffel bags with the rest of the gear on the dock and received a friendly greeting. One old fisherman, tending his nets further along the shoreline, observed them silently with scant curiosity other than that, little attention was paid to the newcomers.

'Back to you and me, sport.' Val was not going to let it go. 'We said this trip would be the perfect time to decide what is going on between us, right?'

'Right.'

'And since it is a proven fact that there is always—*always*, Tommy, a defining moment in everyone's life,' Val declared earnestly, 'this may be our defining moment.'

'Wow! Psychology *and* philosophy, Val, is there no end to your talents?'

'Nope, so what do you say?'

'I say okay, but Val, what I don't get is why you have to be so, well, so analytical about it?'

'Why? I'll tell you why, Tommy. Too many relationships are decided on at a highly emotional time and confirmed for the wrong reasons.'

'Love is love. It's as simple as that.' He shrugged.

'No, it's rarely simple.' Val said emphatically, 'may I tell you something?'

'Go ahead.'

'Ever heard of—*lovesick?*'

'Sure.'

'Well,' Val went on, 'for some people, love itself can be a sickness—an actual sickness, not joyous euphoria, not exhilaration gushing from every pore. For some it can be an actual debilitating, often devastating, sickness.'

'I known about cases like that, that's not us though.'

'No, not us. What I mean is more the norm, two people are thinking with their passions instead of their common sense without considering all the aspects of what it means to be linked forever. They are, in all probably, dissimilar to each other, and many are just that, dissimilar, that can mean they are eventually going to clash. Just ordinary people like us, and God knows, Tommy we are dissimilar. All right—take an ordinary couple, let's call them—'

'Bonny and Clyde?'

'Never mind—these two average, ordinary people decide to get together for the long haul, they are often totally different in temperament, nature, and character with practically nothing in common and what happens? I'll tell you what happens—it all turns to shit!'

'Not all of them.'

'No, not all, but a scary percentage.'

'How about, opposites attract.'

'That old saw, the cry of the truly desperate.' Val paused to let him think about it all and to gather the rest of her thoughts, then went on. 'What I'm saying is — do we really love each other enough for—well, forever.'

'Ah, love—luuuuuve!' Tommy lifted his eyebrows up and down several times mischievously.

'Okay, so that part is fine but—'

Tommy threw her a flabbergasted look.

Val ruffled his hair. 'Settle down, big guy.'

'Fine?'

'Alright,' Val conceded, 'the sex is great, so is being together and all the rest of it but this is for our lifetime. Don't loose sight of the fact that we've had our ups and downs over the past year. I have to be sure of you *and* just as important—I have to be sure of myself.'

'You?'

'Yes, me.'

'Isn't there some kind of test you could take?'

'You mean something out of one of those sappy magazines?' Val laughed at the idea. 'No.'

'Oh, I don't know, maybe you could—'

'No, Tommy, no! Val declared. 'And I asked you to be serious.'

'I am serious. So, no test?'

'No test.'

'Decision time, huh?'

'Exactly,' Val took his face in both her hands. 'We decide to commit or . . . or—go our separate ways.'

'Separate ways?' Tommy nodded slowly, lost the smile and said, 'okay then.'

'So it's agreed?'

'It's agreed.'

One or two of the divers became a little restless at what was turning into a long wait for the launch that was to take them out to the boat from which they would dive the Coral Reef. They could hear music coming from a small cafe across the street.

'What do you think we should do?' One of the people from San Diego asked Spencer.

'We have to wait for the launch,' Spencer said after consulting a carefully itemized itinerary, 'for the launch guy.'

'Hey Jeff!' Another one of those from San Diego, Tony, hollered, 'where are you going?'

'Get something to drink over at that place.' Others began to follow him across the street to the cafe.

'Someone should watch all this stuff.' Spencer called to them.

'Go ahead,' Tommy told him with a friendly grin, 'we'll keep an eye on everything, Spencer, right?'

'Yes, Spencer,' the young man said, 'want me to get you something?'

'Thanks anyway, I'm good.' Val said.

'Sure?'

'We're okay.' Tommy lifted a plastic bottle.

The cafe, although possibly a center of town activity for the younger set, was not crowded. Several of the divers scrambled to the counter while others took tables almost filling the tiny eatery. The jukebox was stocked with old rock and roll and was pretty loud. The owner of the cafe liked it that way. They called out orders after reading from a chalk menu on the wall and they were a little rowdy. The owner was not about to complain, that kind of business was not an every day thing for the small eatery. And when they asked if they could have the music cranked up even louder he said okay. The song playing when they entered was

'Give me that old time rock and roll. They had been in the café for about an hour when Tommy appeared at the entrance to the café and called,

'He's here!'

As they left the café and ran toward the dock and the waiting launch, the words of Crystal Gale's song hung in the air and trailed after them . . .

'Don't take me half the way,'

Two

The launch was moored against the wooden piling with the motor running noisily. They stood there not knowing quite what to do.

'Well, what are you waiting for?' A man in the boat called as he came up from beneath the motor housing to the deck, 'get aboard.'

Two or three of them stepped onto the launch and the others passed, or tossed, the gear to them. After all the gear had been passed down onto the deck, the rest of them crossed over onto the launch. When the boat man was sure everyone was aboard, he gave the two gas levers a sudden jerk. The engines roared to life and the launch began to pull away from the dock.

'Hey, wait for us!

'Hold it, mate!'

Frank and Jack clambered from the back of a truck. They called out their thanks to the trucker and ran to the launch. Tommy made a leap back onto the dock to help them with their gear then tossed it to others on the boat. But the launch drifted too far away for the three on the dock to make it back. The man reluctantly revved the engines into ahead for a minute to get the boat closer. There were still several feet between the dock and the launch but Tommy and the two newcomers didn't wait any longer, they took a run and then a leap, tumbling hard onto the deck. Frank rolled over onto his back then sat up grinning.

'See Jack,' he said grabbing at his friend for a handshake, 'what did I tell you, plenty of time.' Frank looked up at the faces of those standing around him and shouted good-naturedly, 'Giday all!'

The launch surged out into midstream then wallowed slightly when it hit the outer water. Tidal water flowed down from the hook of land jutting out from the coast and gave the launch a bumpy side to side motion. The granite headland of Cape Upstart climbed steeply from the sea with its northern and eastern faces forming an unbroken rocky rampart. Upstart Bay, which they could see more clearly now, appeared less forbidding. With small sandy beaches enclosed by a narrow rocky promontory around which a stiff breeze then hit the launch. Compounded by the speed of the boat the offshore breeze fired spray into the eager faces that gazed expectantly straight ahead.

'There she is!' Someone shouted excitedly. Others joined in with yells and a few cheers.

'Oh, boy!'

'Wow! That's some boat!'

'You beaut!' One of the Aussies bellowed.

A few points off the port bow a grand luxury motor yacht was riding at anchor. She was indeed a beauty, one hundred and fifty feet at the water line—white and gleaming in the lucent rays of the sinking sun. But instead of slowing, the launch rounded the stern of the white and gleaming zenith of sea going luxury and kept on going. The boatman pivoted the wheel slightly and smiled. They turned to watch as the launch headed away from the pleasure craft that they thought they were going to board. Many were still looking behind them when the man shouted over the noise of the engines.

'There she is—that's your ship—that's the *Erehwon*.'

The sun was lower now and starting to set behind them to the west so they were able to see little more than the shape of the vessel riding at anchor. Then, as the launch moved in closer they could see the ship more clearly, a large sailing ship. The boatman secured a line as the launch touched. One after another they climbed a rope ladder that was hanging from the port side. Handing their gear on up to the one ahead as they went. When the last of them was safely aboard the ship the boatman gunned the engine somewhat more than necessary and the launch began to move quickly.

'So, what do we do now?' Jenny said as the launch veered sharply away back toward the land — disappearing in a cloud of spray and imminent nightfall.

'I guess we go find our cabins.' Tommy said.

'Okay by me,' Val yawned, 'I'm so tired I can't keep my eyes open.'

'That goes for me,' Jeff agreed. 'That plane ride from Los Angeles seemed like forever.'

'Yeah, like a whole day.'

'Fourteen hours and thirty five minutes.' Spencer corrected.

They went on to a hatchway facing the stern that was slightly aft of amidships. A solitary oil lamp at the bottom guided them down the steep stairway to the next deck where they stepped into the main cabin.

It was immediately determined that the ship was old and a good deal weather worn and smiles began to fade. Tommy and Val went on to look through the spacious, though hardly luxurious, accommodations. The main below deck area was dominated by a large cabin with a long wooden table, complete with fiddles for rough weather that ran fore and aft up to a bulkhead about midship. It was primarily a mess cabin where all the meals would be taken but it also served as a place to relax with a number of chairs scattered around. In the adjoining Galley, huge blackened pots and pans hung from runners over a great bear of a stove.

Spencer paused for a few minutes to check over some book shelves to which he was naturally drawn. He was the youngest of them, just turned sixteen and notably smart, about go into his first year of a full academic scholarship at U.C.L.A. pegged him as more than unusually bright. He was a little too far from the source of light at the cabin entrance but even in that half light he could see that the books were on all manner of subjects besides navigation and seamanship. Books scores of them, resting on several shelves at the end of a smallish area just forward of mess cabin. On the middle shelf, a huge leather bound, ship's Bible, beside it others with the same elegant binding and gold lettering. 'Hmm,' Spencer murmured, 'interesting.'

'Do you think we're on the right boat?' Val wondered. 'And, where is everybody?'

'It sure is old, Tommy answered, and 'I thought it would be different. Yeah, right, I didn't see anyone on deck.'

'Hello there!' Val called, and then louder, 'hello! Is anyone home?'

'That would be, is any one abroad, Val,'

'Okay, you try it,'

'Sure. Ahoy! Ahoy!' Tommy shouted, 'is anyone aboard?'

No answer.

'I guess they're all ashore.'

'All of them?

'I guess they must be.' Tommy replied shaking his head.

'Jez, this tub must be a thousand years old.' Wally called as he walked back to join them in the main cabin.

'Oh Lord!' A girl's voice sounded from somewhere forward. It was one of the people from San Diego, an annoyingly fastidious young woman named Mary who was now looking into one of the antiquated toilets. 'Oh, my good Lord!' she cried squeamishly.

Tommy reached up to one of the beams. Massive oak timbers that arched across the width of the vessel at every three feet. He slapped it with an open hand sounding a dull thud. 'She seems strong enough though.' He declared.

'Strong enough?' Val questioned.

'Yeah, strong.'

A feeling ran through the divers as they wandered the cabins. The tangible strangeness of the place began to edge its way into them. And the loss of light didn't help, below deck was now quite dark with the coming of night. Wally lit the wick of an oil lamp that was attached to the bulkhead and the area brightened slightly. One of the other guys lit another lamp, and another. Soon there was light throughout the mess cabin and as they moved along to the other areas more lamps were lit. Tenuous and shadowy to be sure, but any light was better than the darkness that it eliminated. Even so, the feeling persisted although nobody said anything. It was a feeling, no more than that really. One thing seemed clear, that it had been a very long time since these quarters had been occupied. But that wasn't it either. The interior of this lower deck was not musty, but the air seemed flat with an almost primary atmosphere as though the air had never been used by anyone before them.

'Here's another bathroom, well not really, just a can.' Tony yelled from further up forward.

'It's called the head, doofus.' Jeff called back.

'Yeah, the head.'

'I guess we better get ourselves set up, for now anyway,' Tommy contended more or less to anyone near him, 'we can fix things up properly when we see someone in the morning, you know, whoever is supposed to take care of us.'

'That would be the Purser,' Mary told him,' he's the officer who takes care of the passengers.'

'Yeah, the Purser.'

Further along the main cabin Alex wiped his moist brow. 'Man,' he said, 'it's hot in here.'

Jeff thought so too. 'Hotter than a whore in church. Hey Dude!' He yelled motioning to one of the others, 'let's open a few of these windows.'

'They're called portholes,' Tony corrected, then added, 'doofus.'

The disappointment of being on such an old boat was discussed and for most of them, quickly disposed of—it is— what it is. There was more exploring to be done. The toilets they discovered, worked quite efficiently. First, the person using it had to pump up the water pressure lever for a moment or two then, when ready, open a valve which would flush the bowl. The shower was another matter however. One of them had to keep pumping while the other showered, so they took turns. Later they discovered that there was an electric pump to do it after all. The water they found, was not salty and again later, they would come to know that the water ran though a simple desalinization system that removed most, if not all, of the salt.

They found that there were plenty of supplies. Next to the galley was a well stocked larder with all the food they could possibly need. Nothing fancy, just plain but wholesome provisions. In another part of the larder, two big gas operated deep freezers were filled with meats, vegetables and such. There was no shortage of eggs or powdered milk and there were oranges for juice and a lot of canned goods. There would be no complaints about the quantity of food but they had no idea of who was going to cook and serve it. They all knew that the trip was a combination of diving with some work on the boat but just what work was entailed was still to be made clear to them.

Before heading to the bunks, they sat around the mess table talking. The letdown of being on board such an old-fashioned boat had vanished and they were now compliantly relaxed on the issue. Most of them were pretty much exhausted but there was still an air of novelty and of course they were getting to know one another. And almost immediately that curious phenomenon that materializes with people in close quarters that were previously unknown to each other—camaraderie. Friendships were swiftly forged. The hours they had known one another quickly began to seem like years, again something that happens in like situations. Personalities and traits became apparent and laughter and some kidding around soon emerged in a setting that was sure to become the norm and factions of the easy-going kind seemed to be forming. Val and Tommy chatted with pretty much everyone at one time or another during the evening. They realized, right off the bat, that Spencer was not only the spearhead of the people from San Diego but a young man of superior intellect. He was fair haired and freckled with a slight build that hardly signified athleticism and yet here he was about to tackle the challenging

17

Great Barrier Reef and was obviously smart enough to be fully aware of what that would entail. Of course that challenge could be said about all of them.

While Spencer stood out among the divers there was another who also did, though not for the same reasons—Glorianna. Tommy and Val had not really noticed her when they were on the dock waiting for the launch. She was perhaps a little older than the others but then again, perhaps not, it was hard to tell. She was not with those from America or anyone else and seemed to be the obligatory loner that was typical of any collection of people—there had to be one. She wore a dark outfit and seemed a little offbeat in manner, soberly polite but somewhat distant. Glorianna had no really discernable accent and yet was, in a way, foreign, with an extraordinarily white face and intense dark eyes. She never said where she was from and no one asked her. Largely what was said among them was in the general course of a natural conversation and in that way information simply drifted out easily as they talked about almost everything besides the 'war stories' they had experienced in diving.

The evening drew to a natural close, by then many of them were pretty tired from travel anyway. They soon headed for bed and the lamps were dimmed. Just forward of midship there were two quite separate sleeping cabins running side by side each with rows of bunks, one at the regular bed level and an upper. One row of bunks was fixed to the starboard side bulkhead of the ship the other was attached to an inside partition that ran down the middle between the two cabins. Each bunk had its own heavy dark green curtain which opened and closed by pulling solid brass rings on even more solid railings.

'I suppose,' the persnickety Mary had said, 'we really should . . .' But she never finished the thought which was that they should separate themselves, males in one cabin and the girls in the other. What happened instead, each of them, simply fell into the nearest bunk where to most, sleep came quickly.

Sometime after midnight a belt buckle began a gentle, sporadic tapping on the curtain railing attached to tommy's bunk. Tommy had selected a lower berth close the entrance of the large cabin with Val in the one above. His eyes opened and he leaned up on one elbow. One of the lamps was moving. The lamp, turned down low, was not one fastened to bulkheads, those had been turned off, and this one was hanging from the overhead. The lamp swayed back and forth. A lazy, leaden motion, back and forth. It would lean to one side for a while then begin its reluctant move back. Tommy watched as the gloomy shadows changed shape around the cabin with each languorous swing of the sparse light. Then he became aware of the muted creaking timbers of the old ship. He got up and crept across the cabin to the bunk where Spencer was sleeping. Tommy woke him by touching his shoulder lightly. Spencer stirred and came awake but not with any kind of start.

'What is it?'

'We're moving. The boat is moving.' Tommy whispered so as not to disturb any of the others.

Spencer sat up. 'Yeah, you're right,' He was silent for a moment feeling the asymmetric motion of the boat. 'You know Tommy, it's funny, and we didn't see anyone, no one.'

'Yeah, but it's not that funny.'

'More like weird, don't you think its weird?'

'Yeah, weird. I guess the crew must have been ashore and came on board before we sailed.'

'Do you think maybe we should go up now and see them, the sailors, you know, someone?'

Tommy thought about it for a moment. 'No, they'll come down here in the morning.'

'Yeah, I guess.'

Tommy returned to his bunk. Spencer went back to sleep almost immediately. Tommy didn't. Beth was also awake. She pulled her curtain back very slowly and looked around the cabin. Her eyes widened and fixed on the swaying lamp but for only a moment. She closed the curtain sharply and covered her head with the blanket.

The *Erehwon* was indeed under way. Even so, she was scarcely moving through the water. A thick fog bank had moved in from the sea shortly before, and now, as though marshaled to escort the ship on its way, the dense murk had turned and was moving in the same direction and at the same dispirited pace as the vessel. In the wheelhouse two weathered, gnarled hands gripped the steering wheel turning it only in slight movements as the vessel glided silently out into deeper water. The ship displayed port red and starboard green navigation lights but the dank, gelatinous fog obscured them as well as the moon and even the brightest of the southern stars. The ships masts and spars dissolved into the bleak nothingness that surrounded her. The *Erehwon* made no wake and the only sound, a hushed swirl of black water astern as the ship eased silently out toward the open sea—to her inescapable destiny—and the fate of all who now sailed with her.

Three

'This blows!'

They were gathered in the early morning light in tight groups a little forward of midship, nearer the front of the ship where the deck rose gradually to the bowsprit. Some talked quietly, subdued and perhaps a little embarrassed, as though they were interlopers and not meant to be there at all. No one had spoken to, or even gone near them although they could clearly see that there were other people on board. They could see movement in the wheel house. And, now and again a tall figure could be seen moving in and out of the area behind the aft superstructure. They had come on deck some little time before, through the hatchway one after another peering around tentatively before emerging. The hatch was really a six foot high and four foot wide double door entrance facing aft that one stepped inside before descending the companionway that led down to the deck below.

'This,' Jeff declared petulantly, 'really blows.'

'Patience is a virtue,' Mary told him sagely.

'Oh, really?'

'Yes,' she confirmed then finishing the proverb, 'patience is a virtue, possess it if you can, always found in women, never in a man.' And with that she threw him a demure, though hardly heartfelt, smile.

'Is that so? It still blows.'

Most of those on deck seemed to agree with Jeff. They stood or moved around self-consciously in small groups, not knowing what to do and looking from time to time, at the wheel house. Wondering what they might do other than what they were doing which was nothing and feeling a little foolish. They could see, through the window of the wheelhouse that someone was in there steering the ship, which was barely under way. There was a light breeze that was coupled with a low swell giving some movement to the ship. Tommy thoughtfully glanced to the West. With the steadily raising sun at his back, he could see the coast not more than three or four miles away from their position. The ship seemed to be moving, if moving at all, parallel to the shoreline. In fact she was moving against the current and the small sails on the ship made up for the leeway meaning that the ship was actually staying in about the same place.

'What the hell, we can't just stand around like this all day?' Tony exclaimed.

Some of the others began to voice opinions similar to him and Jeff. But the Australians of them, just shrugged if off.

'They'll tell us something soon, I guess.' Wally thought.

'We're hungry,' Debbie wailed, 'I wonder where the cook is, there has to be a cook. Doesn't there have to be a cook?'

'Why don't you go down to the galley and get yourself something,' Spencer suggested, 'I did, there's plenty of food down there.'

Jeff had an idea. 'Hey, the chicks should go fix breakfast.'

'Fix your own, big shot,' Debbie said, 'come on Mary, Val, you coming?'

'You bet.'

Just about everyone was about to go below but stopped when they heard a clatter from the wheel house. The hatch swung open sharply banging against the side of the housing. The noise, although not all that loud, startled them into immobility for a moment. Apart from the light, even swell the sea was quite calm and the vessel was under the lightest of sailing rigs, just one small sail on the mainmast and a much smaller one on the mizzen. A jury rig, just enough canvas for the vessel to make way and no more. The commonplace sound of a door opening seemed to have more effect on them than it would have under other circumstances. All eyes turned in that direction.

A hand tied down the wheel with a rope that was there for that purpose and a man came through the door. He was tall with gaunt features covered by a lined and weathered skin. His eyes, heavily hooded by gray-white brows, were languid and dark as midnight. An Asian man of a dark complexion and a bald head followed just behind him. He was not quite as tall as the man he followed but he was nevertheless, a giant of a man. His legs and arms had great bulging muscles that glistened like metal in the morning sun. The only thing small about him was his head, joined to a neck that thickened as it became part of the massive shoulders, his arms, tree trunks. Tony stepped forward a little.

'Hi, can you . . .?'

The man ignored Tony and walked quickly past him and the others without a glance. The Asian man then moved ahead of him to the forward deck superstructure to the fo'c'sle hatchway. He opened the heavy lock with a key and went in through the hatch and down the steps inside. He reappeared soon after pushing another man ahead of him.

He was small with a graying beard and matted hair. The clothes he wore were rumpled and he staggered a little. The big man followed close behind. The strange trio moved on up to stop just in front of the wheelhouse where the man in front turned to face the other two. He nodded to the Asian man who, in answer to what was a silent order, slung a bucket with a rope attached over the side and hauled it in when it was full and quickly dashed the bearded man with sea water. The smaller man staggered and was nearly knocked from his feet and but moved back to the same spot to receive another bucketful of water. The bucket was refilled and the process repeated one more time.

'Look alive, Mister, you have the watch at four bells.'

The small man glared at him but stood more or less erect seemingly trying to shake off the effects of what might be a month long bender and produced a loud hacking cough before being able to speak.

'Aye, aye, captain.'

The captain turned his attention to the others on deck.

'Ship's company,' he said in a voice that was not all that loud but could be heard clearly by everyone on deck, 'allow me to introduce you to Mister Quigley.' He looked them over for a minute before continuing. 'Mister Quigley is the First Officer of this ship.'

A few murmurs and one or two audible chortles followed this announcement. Without the slightest raising of his voice the captain continued. 'You will take note of what I just called you— ships company.' He began to walk away from them then turned for a last word. 'You should also be mindful that the First Officer of this vessel, the First Officer of any vessel, is to be accorded the respect due to his station.'

The captain then walked aft and disappeared inside the wheel house.

That afternoon found many of them gallivanting around the ship like a bunch of clowns. These had decided that the whole trip was pretty much a bust. Tommy, Val and Spencer along with some of the others including a couple of the Aussies were more rational about the situation. But they too had to concede that the trip gave every appearance now of being a washout. Tommy tried to talk to Quigley, but had been met with stony silence or a vacant stare. Not one syllable came out of the man's mouth. The same thing occurred when he tried to engage the big Asian fellow, nothing.

No doubt, things would have been different had they been able to dive. But there was no diving simply because the ship was moving, and even though it was only moving slowly people can't dive off an unanchored vessel and since diving was the reason for the trip it was easy for them to conclude that it was a bust. A relatively small number of them thought to hell with it—let's just have what fun we can. It was hot, the weather clear and the sea calm and they were the ones who were at the age where almost constant activity is essential. They played improvised volley ball but soon tiring of that turned to more senseless capers. Even the sun bathers when asked to join in—some, perhaps in the spirit of fellowship, felt obliged to do so. Glorianna was nowhere to be seen and since she seemed to be not the jauntiest of people, was not missed.

The captain was not on deck and had not been since the first mate, Quigley had taken over the wheel house. The Asian man seemed to go about whatever he was doing and like Quigley, ignored them. The deck was soon a mess. Food was trampled, cans littered and rolled around. The middle and fore decks were a shambles. In the galley and main cabin there was evidence also of their mindless spree. In one day they had turned the ship into a floating junk heap. Even in the sleeping cabins clothes and trash lay on unmade bunks. Blaring music screeched ceaselessly. They felt frustrated and cheated; they had expected some great diving and instead were stuck on an old boat just a few miles from the shore.

Val and Tommy were sort of in the middle of things. Not wanting to appear to be too high and mighty yet it was against their nature to be destructive just for the fun of it. They just minded their own business and lazed around in the sun for most of the day with those of a like mind.

Mary definitely set herself apart from what she considered to be outright vandalism. Going so far as to set a place for herself at the extreme end of the table at the late meal that each fixed for themselves. And when a food fight broke out she left the cabin altogether and took her carefully prepared plate to the privacy of her bunk. She closed the curtain and remained there for the rest of the night.

Spencer just naturally, buried himself in the ship's library for the day and most of the evening. Actually he didn't mind that at all. It gave him a chance to check out the most of the books. He could quite rightly be called a bookworm and that was true but Spencer was by no means a nerd. He was an excellent diver and a good sport that could mix it up with the best of them.

Jeff was in his element coming, as he did, from the stilted confines of a rather controlling family. He was enjoying the situation more than anyone else, belting out 'dude! and 'excellent!' all over the place.

'Look at him,' Jenny said turning to Laura, 'like a kid and strutting around like he owns the fucken ship.'

The Australians, in their idiomatic cant, called him a larrikin. Jeff asked Frank what it meant.

'A larrikin? Well, he's like, you know—a larrikin.'

'Yeah, and?'

'Like, well a larrikin is a bloke who's full of piss and vinegar, like always up to something, you get it mate?'

'Yeah, I get it' Jeff thought about it for a minute. 'Yeah, that's me alright, I am the larrikin!'

'Yeah, well,' Frank explained, 'it's *a* larrikin not *the* larrikin.'

But Jeff was adamant.

'Oh no dude, no, no! I am *the* larrikin!'

Even with all of the shenanigans the night came to a rather dreary end with pretty much all of them going to their bunks rather tired, the Aussies called it *buggered,* and the Americans said *bushed.*

Nothing stirred for the rest of the night.

Four

Clang! Clang! Clang!

A deafening noise clattered through the sleeping quarters, through the lower deck, not to mention the rest of the ship, breaking the almost total silence of seconds before. The only sounds previously had been the creaking timbers of the vessel and some light snoring coming from someone at the forward end of the sleeping cabins. Quigley swung a long steel spoon onto a big cooking pan over and over again, making an incredibly loud racket—somewhere between a fractured alarm bell and a jackhammer. He stopped bashing the pan to shout in a commanding voice.

'Captain's orders! All you people get on deck in five minutes! Five minutes!' Then he started up with the banging again as he moved from one cabin to the other and back again.

'Out of them bunks now! Whatever shape you're in, move!'

Clang! Clang! Clang!

'Deaf, dumb, lazy, blind drunk or crazy,' he yelled, 'get up outta them bunks!'

Clang! Clang! Clang!

'On your feet!'

He moved to the doorway of the main cabin and shouted the more formal order.

'All hands on deck!'

'What the hell's he yelling?' Tony asked.'

'Who knows?' Wally said, 'all I got was we have to get up on deck'

'Holy shit! What time is it?'

'You kidding? It's still night!

'It's a quarter to five.'

Quigley looked a little on the eccentric side but presented far different character than that of the day before. He was wearing a brass buttoned dark blue tunic and an officers cap. His shoes were shined and he wore a clean blue shirt buttoned up at the neck with no tie. His face was not clean shaven but the matted, dirty facial hair of the day before was gone replaced by a fairly trim pepper and salt beard. His demeanor was also different. He stood up straight and moved with a well-balanced, almost military bearing.

'All hands on deck!' He shouted one last time as he barreled up the companionway stairs.

One after another they dragged themselves up on deck. Half dressed and moody, many wore the swimsuits and shorts that they had on the night before. They squinted in the peculiar pre-dawn light. Quigley lined them up into a less than straight pattern facing the stern of the ship. Moving rapidly along the line he pushed and pulled them into some order. When he was satisfied that this was the best he could do he walked smartly to the wheel house, touched his cap in salute and spoke in a respectful manner.

'All present and standing to on deck, captain.'

Quigley stood back and a little to one side. The captain stepped into a position facing them. The big Asian followed him.

There were a few murmurs which the ship's master silenced with no more than a glance. He looked them over from one end of the line to the other.

'Ship's company,' he waited a few moments before continuing apparently to be certain that he had their attention. 'My name is Burke, Captain Burke, the deck upon which you now stand is that of the good ship *Erehwon*. The *Erehwon* is a top'sil schooner—a sailing vessel.' Captain Burke paused for a moment in both walk and talk, to look carefully at one or two of them, and then went on with both the information and the stroll along the deck.

'Now then, you just heard me call you the ship's company, Mister Quigley is the first mate that means he is second in command of the vessel. This man,' he pointed at the big Asian, 'is the bos'un, his name is Sulkar, and he is to be addressed as bos'un. Then you, all of the rest of you, make up the ship's company, the crew.' He held up a sheet of paper. 'Here are your provisional assignments. Each member of the ship's company is assigned the job he is to do.'

Captain Burke let all that he had said sink in while he walked back down the line. This time he took a long, thoughtful, look into the face of each of them, almost as though he were trying to register every feature of the face before moving on to the next person.

'At this time, in addition to that job every crew member will attend to the first order, which is cleaning. The vessel is to be cleaned from stem to stern, and it is to be cleaned to Bristol fashion.'

Tommy glanced at Val who opened her eyes wide and mouthed the words, *'what about the diving?'*

The captain moved back to the center of the deck in front of the wheelhouse and favored them with a long stare.

'A cautionary note,' he went on, 'you should be mindful that orders are just that, orders. On this vessel orders will be issued only once. You would do well to understand that.'

'What the hell is Bristol fashion?' Jeff muttered.

'Attention on deck!' Quigley barked, 'no talking!'

The captain went on.

'Mister Quigley and the bos'un will instruct you in your duties and seamanship, look to them when you are not sure. Do what the First Officer and the Bos'n tell you to do. A number of you to be instructed in navigation.'

He held up a book for them all to see.

'To inform you on any matter that might arise at sea. Forget anything you may think you know as law. There is land law and there is sea law. This is the ship's book of Maritime Law. We follow only this book. The law of the sea.'

Val looked at Tommy 'Hmmm?'

Tommy shrugged.

'Mister Quigley!'

'Aye, captain?'

'Set them their tasks.'

'Aye, aye sir.'

On the way to the lower deck Tommy asked Val what she thought about all the things they had heard.

'I guess that's the way it's done on a ship.'

'Yeah, I guess so.' Tommy agreed. 'We knew half the trip is supposed to be about work.'

'Well, yes, but the other half was for the diving, he never mentioned the diving, and when does that part come in?'

'When indeed? It looks like we're supposed to do whatever there is to do on a sailing ship like this, that is if there is any another ship like this one which I am inclined to doubt.'

'And you, no lawyering muscle here, is that legal emasculation?'

'So what? This is vacation time, right?'

'Right—and time for the talk.'

'Ah, the talk. Of course, Val, of course.'

Below, in the main cabin between the galley and the section that leads to the companionway up to the deck, they crowded around Quigley as he posted the assignment list on the bulkhead near the galley door. It was written clearly in a meticulous, old-fashioned handwriting.

'Okay, okay,' Alex said, 'let's see who does what, hey, quit pushing!'

'Hey, Alex!' Tony called. 'What did I get?'

'Why don't you read them out?' Someone yelled.

Tommy could see the list above Alex's head.

'Okay let's see,' Tommy said, 'ah, I got seaman and Navigation,' he nudged Spencer, 'you got ship's clerk.'

'Deck hand?' Debbie said, 'me a deck hand?'

'You're lucky,' one of the girls cried, 'look what I got, galley hand! I'm a goddamned galley slave!'

'Me too,' Val said, 'I have to work in the galley, and Midshipman.'

'That should be Midshipwoman.' The vexingly precise Mary said.

'I'm a mess hand,' Jim said, 'and seaman.'

Mary seemed pleased when she read what job she had been assigned. 'That's fine, I'm a very good cook, and I like cooking.'

'What's A B? There are a lot of them, hey, what's an A B?' Alex asked Quigley.

'A B means Able Bodied Seaman.' He told them.

'Why did the he say provisional assignments?' Val wanted to know.

'We got to see what you can do, what kind of stuff you're made of, what kind of salt you got,'

'Salt?'

'Like how good ya are at the job, that's how much salt ya got.'

'Yes, I see Mister Quigley,' Val said, 'and tell me, what exactly is a Midshipman?'

'Now that's a real smart question that is, awwwright, see, there's the officers, like the captain and me, then there's the sailors, right?'

'Uh huh?'

'So a Midshipman is in between, mid he's not an officer and not a sailor, he's a Midshipman. It's from the old days and it had to do with where their births were, where they bunked, Midshipmen was in the middle lower deck of them old navy sailing ships. Awwwright, now, everyone to work, ya got a job to do.'

'Boat puller? I got boat puller?' Jeff looked at Quigley.

'Maybe you have to pull the boat.' Alex said.

'What about breakfast,' one of them shouted, 'we can't work without food?'

'Another good question that is,' Quigley said, 'well ain't you the clever swabbies,'

'What the hell are swabbies?' Wally asked.

'You are. Swabbies is new sailors,'

'So how about it, breakfast?'

'Yeah food, Quigley' Wally said.

'That would be Mister Quigley or just Mister will do, you got it boy?'

'Yeah, got it.'

'Got it?'

'Got it . . . Mister Quigley.'

'Awwwright now! 'Quigley shouted, 'you cooks, galley hands and mess hands get yourselves into the galley and mess now.'

Nobody moved.

'Now!' Quigley shouted.

Val, Mary and the two who had the galley duties began moving into that area and those who were not, and in their way, were shoved aside by Quigley.

'When the food is ready, you eat it, how soon you get it is up the galley hands. The meal times list will be posted later when we set the watches, some of you will eat at different times according to your duties and what watch you will be on. All that will be sorted out as we go along. From tomorrow breakfast will be at five-thirty, work starts at six.'

'Holy crap, five thirty?'

'Aye, we turn to late on this ship.'

'How about us, the galley people,' Val said, 'what time do we have to get out there?'

'Five if you prepare good the night before.'

There was a break in the questions so Jeff steered Quigley aside from the rest for a private word.

'See, here's the thing, Quigley,' He said

'Mister Quigley.'

'Whatever, see I've been around boats a lot, and I know a lot, my dad has a boat himself, a new boat, not like this old tub of shit, and see I have a lot of skills, so I don't want that boat puller thing.'

'So you know what boat puller does then?'

'Oh yeah, sure,'

'Skills? And you have skills?'

Jeff nodded vigorously. 'You bet!'

'I see, hmmmm, well then,' Quigley scratched his chin thoughtfully, 'any suggestions?'

'Well yeah, you could make me, you know, an officer,'

'Officer?'

'Yeah.'

'Hmm, couldn't be right away you know that might take a couple of days and I'm afraid only the captain can do that.'

'You could talk to him, right?'

'Hmm, I could I suppose …' Quigley scratched his chin.

'Well okay, maybe not an officer right off, maybe some kind of specialist, you know?'

'A specialist, well now, if you're like a specialist, I suppose yes, that would make a difference, and say later an officer, how does that sound?'

'Now you're talking,'

'Awwwright then' Quigley said brightening, 'I got a specialists job for you then, awwwright, and you are not boat puller.'

Quigley turned back to the others to answer questions about the various duties and to explain what they would be doing. Jeff took Tony to one side.

'Hey Tony,' he said with a nod and a wink, 'see, you have to be firm with these jerks, you can't let them push you around, if there's any pushing to be done I'm going to be the one doing the pushing, that's for sure.'

'Awwwright now then!' Quigley announced stridently, 'Cooks, galley and mess hands turn to right away, the rest of you have ten minutes to get yourself dressed for the deck, be on deck in that time, now go!'

As he turned he brushed past Tony.

'You boy, you are now boat puller.'

'Shit!'

Jeff shook his head in fake sympathy adding several 'tsk tsks,' and ended the taunt with a couple of juvenile heehaws. Before the meeting ended Tommy asked the question that was paramount for all of them.

'What about diving, Mister Quigley, I mean, when will we get to do any diving?'

'That's something the captain will tell you.'

'Well, we'd like to know when and do we dive here where we are now?'

'Not here, we have to sail further up the reef, that's where we got to go to the long reef.'

'But—'

'The captain will say where and when.'

The mess they had made themselves had to be cleaned up. And in fact that really didn't take too long, all done by the noon hour. For the most part they were pretty pleased with themselves when it was done. They stood by confidently as Quigley went from place to place around the deck in what they thought was a final inspection. The ship had moved a little north in the night to the shelter of a large cove that was not really part of the headland, just a fairly low piece of coastal land that offered placid water. The anchor had been dropped and the light sailing rig had been furled. She was riding effortlessly at anchor a few miles off the coast which was on two sides with the open sea to the north east just around the spit.

'What do you say Mister Quigley,' Wally said, 'not too bad?'

'Not too bad? Hmmm, not too bad ain't too good, neither.' He gave them a long look and a shake of his head.

'Awwwright now, pick up them buckets and them mops and them scrubbers and let's get to work.'

The cleaning of the ship, to Quigley's satisfaction, took the rest of that day and half of the next. The first mate and the bos'n urged them on every minute of those long days. There was nothing that got by Quigley from the tiniest scrap of muck on one of the bollard keepers to scouring the specks of seabird fouling in the scuppers. Nothing above the deck itself was touched however, that is to say the sails and rigging, all of which was in apparently good order. And anyway at that time they, the crew, knew nothing about that part of the ship to any extent. Even the ships bell was cleaned by Jim to shine like brass had never shined before.

Below deck in the galley, main cabin and sleeping quarters everything was cleaned with all the equipment stowed in it's proper place. They began to think that the lower deck began to look rather special. Spencer, the ship's clerk, opened records on everything from inventorying the food stores on board to the proper planning of meal times and anything else that had to do with the day to day running of a ship. As ship's clerk he felt that it was his job to see that it all ran smoothly. As expected, he was meticulous in his approach to the whole operation and it was the kind of work he enjoyed.

'Why bother?' Tommy asked him. 'We'll only be on the boat for a short time, is it worth the trouble?'

'Probably not, but you know the old saying, if a job is worth doing it's worth doing well.'

'He's got a point, Tommy.' Val said.

Tommy shrugged. 'Uh huh, I guess.'

By the end of that first day of cleaning, the ship overall was starting to shape up. Their attitude, if they had time to think about it, was not really that bad. Sure, there was some bitching about not getting right into the diving. But in the end they did the job that they were told to do and never complained openly to any great extent, except of course for Jeff. He asked Quigley several times when exactly he would get off the cleaning detail and start his specialist job only to be told, to be patient. Even if there was not that much complaining the fact remained that this was certainly not the trip they had envisioned or signed on for. There was up to now, no diving and no sailing either. However, there were other things that kept them relatively lighthearted. The question: 'When do we get to do some diving?' was asked of Quigley many times with the same answer, 'When the captain ses so.'

And Val had a question of her own.

'Tommy,' Val pulled him aside from the others for a private word, 'I may have found the perfect place for us to talk—'

'Talk?'

'Don't play dumb, you know what I mean.'

'Oh, yeah . . . the talk.'

'It's up in front of the sleep and mess cabins. You know something, it looks like this ship might have once been in service of some kind for real passengers. There are several cabins, very small cabins, tiny in fact, but they look like they haven't been used for a long time. We can maybe sneak into one of them, what do you think?'

Tommy brightened. 'Uh ha!'

'Stop it, you know what I mean, well yeah that too—maybe. What I meant was a place where we can talk about you know what. We are never really alone.'

'Oh, yeah, okay, but right now we have a lot of this stuff to do and—'

'Don't try to wriggle out of it Tommy, you promised.'

'Of course Val, of course. But not right now, okay? we'll get to it don't worry, just as soon as we can, you bet.'

'Okay, then.'

The cooks, Mary, Kim and Joey quickly fell into a solid routine of rotating duties as did the mess and galley hands. The food was good, and there was plenty of it so there was no grumbling on that score. Besides, they had their off duty time together in the evenings and nights and friendships quickly strengthened. They were, in fact, appreciating each others company. Especially in the way the Americans became buddies with the Aussies who in turn were their mates. Matthew, the very well spoken Englishman, got on well with all of them as did the young man from Hong Kong, Siu Ming. Oh, from time to time there were minor disagreements but these were quickly resolved and forgotten. Glorianna was the quiet one and pretty much kept to herself when not on duty with others. No doubt the work was hard and tiring but like it or not they were starting to enjoy themselves against their first instinct which was not to do so. Of course. They were anxious to start diving but that was something to look forward to which they did with huge anticipation all round.

Those first days when the sun began to dip to the horizon Quigley would dismiss them and they were off duty to do more or less as they pleased. There was however, no more of the behavior of that first day. They had learned that lesson the hard way. The crew, perhaps instinctively, seemed, to settle into a solid routine that suited pretty much everyone.

'Hey,' Laura called to those near her, 'the coastline is on the other side now.'

'We're swinging on the anchor,' Tommy told her pointing to the land, 'swinging with the tides.'

'It sucks,' Jeff bellyached. 'When the hell are we going to move off to the diving place of the reef?'

'Get back to it, Jeff.' Wally warned, 'Quigley's coming, he'll tear you a new one if he sees you goofing off.'

'Like I give a shit. Crazy asshole, *'bend to it now,'* Jeff mimicked with a fair imitation of Quigley's irritating voice.

'Come along lads, bend to it now!' Quigley said for about the tenth time before moving on.

'Crazy asshole.'

'Maybe so, but he's probably a good seaman,' Tony said joining the conversation, 'we can learn a lot from him, I mean a lot.'

'This sure is some vacation, huh?' Jeff grouched and shook his head, 'some vacation, sprucing up this old crap heap scow.'

Most of them however felt differently. While doing the cleaning they began to take some pride in their work. That made things easier on all of them. With each job accomplished the *Erehwon* became a different ship and there was no doubt it was from the second day, a different crew.

Captain Burke didn't come on deck during the day at all. But they could sometimes see him in the wheel house at night when they would be relaxing on deck. The days were extremely hot but the nights were nothing short of prefect and downright balmy. They spent the evenings, after they had eaten the last meal of the day and freshened up, on the middle and forward decks. Talking and gazing at the stars that came right down to the horizon in every direction. The second night on board the *Erehwon* the moon was in the lower quadrant and couldn't be seen, bright stars covered the entire sky coming down to the horizon in every direction. The air was so clean around them and with no other light to interfere, the furthermost stars in the solar system and beyond radiated light with brilliance that none of them had ever seen before. And set in the milky way, the Great Southern Cross, the longer arm of which pointed, perhaps prophetically, south and blazed down on them with the luminescence of four beckoning beacons.

'Hey Tommy!' Wally called as he came out of the bunk cabin and into the mess holding a player, 'look no batteries.'

'Yeah, I know, all the batteries are gone.' Tommy called back from the door of the galley where he had been talking to Val as she worked with Kim and Mary on the breakfast preparation.

'Mine too, what gives?' Beth asked indignantly, 'how are we going to get any music?'

'We're not, I guess.' Val said as she watched Mary crack another egg and drop it into a pan where several more were sizzling to perfection.

'What gives,' another of them, Frank said as he entered 'what the hell's going on here?'

Tommy was less concerned than the others and Spencer didn't care that much either even though he, like the others, enjoyed most music, but that was not why he came on the trip, if there was music fine, if there was not that was fine too.

'I suppose it's because there was too much noise.' Tommy told them.

'No doubt about it.' Spencer agreed.

'Well I don't mind at all,' Mary affirmed as she jiggled bacon strips in a huge pan, 'there was altogether too much rowdiness anyway.'

Jeff rolled his eyes.

'There was!' Mary insisted.

'Sons of bitches.' Jeff said, disgusted and some of the others voiced similar sentiments with a variety of colorful language

It was Mary's turn to roll her eyes. She slammed the pan onto the stove with a wallop that made the bacon slices jump.

Five

'All hands on deck!'

Spencer was working at the little desk in the cramped area that was his office. This alcove abutted the maim cabin but was quite separate because of a bulkhead between that and the mess cabin. Despite the scarcity of space, it afforded him a reasonably good work station. He heard the call but paid no attention to it. Then on thinking about it, Quigley's order was clear enough, 'all hands on deck' did mean all hands. Yet, he still didn't go up. Instead he went to the end of the main cabin. To the bookshelves. He found the book he wanted and pulled it out from the shelf, in doing so another volume fell. He picked it up and read the title, Mariners Prayers. Spencer was about to put it back but changed his mind. He took it back to the little office. He heard Quigley's call again. 'All hands on deck!' More insistent this time.

Spencer dropped the book on his desk and made his way through to the companionway and up the stairs to the middle deck. He found that the captain was about to begin his inspection. Those on deck stood at the stations that Quigley had assigned them a few minutes before. The captain made a cursory turn around the deck and seemed to them, rather disinterested but in fact he had kept himself apprised of all that had been going on and didn't need any more than a quick glance.

There was another entrance to the lower deck that led down through to an area behind the galley. The captain followed Quigley as he opened the deck door and went down to do the same with the door at the bottom of the stairwell. There were rails on each side of the stairs that allowed the nimble Quigley to skate on down with little effort, his feet scarcely touching the steps. But the captain went down in the normal manner easing on down and in through the main cabin at a deliberate pace, then the galley and sleeping quarters. He touched nothing and said not a word to the first mate but little escaped his eye. The inspection although thorough, was done in a relatively short time and the captain made his way back to the deck in the same way he had descended, this time Quigley followed closing both doors behind him. Once on deck Captain Burke glanced briefly at the people standing by.

'Report, Mister Quigley,' he said.

'A one and Bristol fashion, as ordered, the ship is ready for sea.'

'Very well.' He looked up at the sky for a moment. 'Yes, the ship is ready for sea. Very well Mister, you may secure and stand by for my orders.'

'Aye, aye sir.'

Captain Burke positioned himself in his customary place in front of the wheelhouse, Quigley, a respectful few feet behind and to one side. The Bos'n, Sulkar stood, arms folded on the upper fore deck. Everyone else was in a ragged line more or less facing the captain. When he spoke it was in rather a subdued voice but there was no doubt as to the authority behind the words.

'Mister Quigley, make all preparations for getting under way.'

'Aye, aye, sir.'

Quigley grouped three of the crew and pushed them in front of him.

'You three, go forward and stand by the cable rig and wait for orders from the Bos'n, you, come with me, you two up there!' He pointed. 'You, you and you, stand by the shroud lines and wait for orders, you and you, to the afterdeck and stand by, move!'

And move they did—but to little purpose. It became nothing more than a chaotic scurrying, in which everyone seemed to run around—or simply barge into one another. There seemed to be no sense to what the first mate was doing in sending them in almost every direction to do what they had no idea.

'Not that way!' Sulkar said as he grabbed Jim by the shirt and britches and turned him effortlessly around on the dead run from fore to aft. Wally and Alex went to the middle deck as ordered, and then stood anxiously at the bottom of the port rope ladder leading up the mainmast.

'What are you waiting for? Up!' Quigley ordered.

Wally followed by Alex scrambled ungainly up the rigging to the first yard arm and looked down to Quigley who then crossed his forearms with fists clenched indicating that they should hold at that point.

'Bos'n!' Captain Burke called through cupped hands, 'weigh anchor!'

Sulkar set several youngsters to turning the capstan which wasn't that hard really with four of them turning but they were not coordinated with each other and they got it a few turns but it turned the other way making them back up—they had to start all over again. Tommy, with some of the others, hauled on a rope that began to hoist the mainsail.

'Pull together now, pull!' Quigley bellowed.

Someone let it slip and they fell to the deck and like the others trying to raise the anchor, had to start all over again.

The *Erehwon* lay leaden in the water with no indication that she was going to move. There was a lot of noise and yelling from the crew and orders from Quigley and Sulkar but there was no sign that the ship was going anywhere. Alex made a mistake that could have been costly, losing his grip in trying to loosen a rope on the yardarm, he plunged downward but was caught in the rope netting placed there by Quigley. He was unhurt except for his pride as several of the others derided his graceless fall and gawky efforts to extricate himself from the netting. A couple of the others in the end helped him down.

Remarkably perhaps, but finally after a lot of effort and a good deal more frustration, the main sail was hoisted and another sail forward of the main mast, dropped into position. The anchor was weighed and secured and they felt the deck move slightly under their feet. The bow lifted a little and began to move through the water. Scarcely moving but the *Erehwon* was under way.

'Starboard watch! On deck!'

'Oh no, not again?'

'Four times today already,' Beth, one of the seven of them that were on the starboard watch, groaned.

'On deck, me lads!' Quigley called from the top of the companionway steps.

'Hey! Mister Quigley,' Frank shouted back, 'my friggin' hands are cut raw from those ropes!'

'On deck, look lively,' Quigley shouted again, 'I've got some brine for those hands boy.'

'Excellent,' Frank retorted, 'why don't you just go ahead and shove it up your ass!'

'Well you're startin' to talk like a sailor, anyway.' Quigley called back.

The crew had been setting sails, then furling sails, then resetting sails again and yet again. Tacking to leeward, tacking to windward, running with the wind and tacking against the wind. There had been no let up, day and night for three days. The crew had been divided into three watches, and many of the duties were now on an unpredictable rotation so erratic that some of those who were doing one job were assigned another and then on again to another and back again. It was all very unsettling but they were learning an awful lot about sailing and running a ship.

Jeff had what looked like was going to be his permanent job. He had pestered Quigley one time too many about the specialist job he would get, hoping of course, that it would be a cushy one, wrong. He was given a part of the deck to recondition. The uppermost fore deck. Just a small section of deck really but one that caught a good deal of the weather over the years and the teak planking was greatly tarnished. The job was the Praying Stone, sometimes called the Holy Stone. Jeff had to get down on his knees and push a ten pound block of lime stone back and forth to scrape the years of grime off the wood down to the original grain. He had to keep the stone consistently wet with sea water and that added another discomfort to what was already tough work. When Jeff thought the job was done Quigley told him, 'do it again.'

When Jeff was finished for the third time Quigley repeated, 'do it again.'

'The whole friggin' thing?'

'The whole friggin' thing.'

'Okay then, just don't forget our deal.'

'Oh, I aint forgettin' nothin'.'

The Holy Stone was known by old sailors as the worst job one could get aboard ship, and the one that was usually turned over to sailors as a punishment for some infringement of regulations. Quigley had not overlooked Jeff's remark referring to the *Erehwon* as 'an old tub of shit,' that, and his cockiness, had earned him the job. Adding salt to the wound, Tony didn't let him forget that he had weaseled his way out of his first assignment of Boat Puller. The irony was of course, that Boat Puller turned out to be the about the best job on board, looking after the Long boat. The work required Tony to keep the boat in good order, to see to it that the boat was fully provisioned with sea rations and fresh water in the event of an emergency, and check that the compass on the boat was in good working order. The boat, which was lashed on top of the superstructure on the middle deck, was large but Tony was surprised and of course tickled, to find it was in excellent condition, being as it was at all times covered with a heavy tarpaulin. It was equipped with a collapsible mast and boom which could be rigged in a few minutes when needed. The long boat had a main sail and a smaller jib and was equipped with a spare for both and a compass that was built into a rostrum in front of the tiller. All the bright work, the brass rollicks, bushings and so forth on the longboat were unsoiled and the rows of benches were varnished to an absolute brilliance.

Although quite large, the long boat was easily launched, first it was swung out on divots then lowered by the attached ropes into the water. There was very little that Tony had to do but check everything each day, a little light polishing and secure the tarpaulin when he was finished. From his perch inside the boat atop the superstructure, Tony could see Jeff on the fore deck. Down on his knees, the sweat running down his shirtless back, pushing the Praying Stone back and forth. Tony made up a few words, parodying Jeff's shifty maneuver, to the song, Drift Away that went, 'so if there's any pushing to be done I'm the guy going to do it, 'la-de-da.' Jeff looked back at him menacingly but Tony only quit the singing when Quigley came around and stopped altogether when it got old anyway.

As well as the other jobs like cook, mess hand, clerk to which they had been assigned, each were part of the three watches, starboard, port and middle and were required to rush to the deck when that watch was called upon. After a few days things began to settle down and into place and calls to the deck became less frequent and finally, infrequent. They went about their jobs, which with routine became easier all the time. Therefore they had a measure of spare time to do whatever they wanted—they began to enjoy life aboard a sailing ship.

Curiously, Tommy was enjoying the work as much as anyone on the ship. Not only was he using muscles that had pretty much lay dormant during his years of study for the law, his mind was accruing a varied amount of knowledge. And he was out on the ocean. Lecture halls and dusty law libraries had till now, been his milieu.

Val liked the change of pace too, perhaps not as much as Tommy and for different reasons. She found that she was able to appreciate the company of her crew mates, people who were more inclined to have fun rather than her colleagues and classmates back home who were generally of a more serious caliber. And, without thinking that much about it, observe a multiplicity of characters among them.

Quigley was finally satisfied with the work on the fore deck and Jeff was reassigned to seaman and was also required to take the navigation instruction along with Val, Tommy, Spencer and Wally. Quigley complimented Jeff with his work on the deck and told him it was the best Holy Stone job he had ever seen.

'Well damn me, you are a specialist.' He snickered.

Jeff was, notwithstanding all his complaining, pleased with himself and his work. So pleased that in his spare time, when in the normal course of events, being Jeff, he would just goof off, instead he made a small brass plaque that he engraved with tools provided by the first mate. It was only about three by five inches but he did an excellent job of it. He asked Quigley if he could screw it onto the fore deck and received permission to do so. Written on the little brass plate,

'The Larrikin's Deck'

Those days and nights could not be called fun. The hard labors endured by the crew, climbing into the rigging, pulling on lines, with Quigley and Sulkar shouting orders, dragging themselves from their bunks and then falling back onto them exhausted was hardly pleasurable. However, toward the end of those first few days instead of the stumbling around the crew now seemed to have found their sea legs and Quigley seemed to be satisfied—with him it was hard to tell—but now and then he would nod indicating approval of a job or the rigging and furling work.

The captain instructed them in longitudes, coastal, ocean and celestial navigation, compass headings and the like. How to read charts and maps, to use plotters and other navigational equipment such as shooting the sun with the sextant. Tommy, Val, and Spencer were among those in his navigation class who proved to be the most interested and therefore the most adept. They were learning a lot and learning fast. Tacking and maneuvering become almost second nature to everyone. They were now getting the 'feel' of the vessel. Reefing and setting sails, splicing and rigging. Better than any classroom, they were learning by doing. All under the supervision of the mate, Quigley, who, although clearly a drunkard when ashore and possibly a crackpot at sea, they could see that the cackling first mate knew what he was about in every manner of seamanship. But still there was no diving and there didn't seem to be any immediate plans for the diving to start. Remarkably there was less grumbling about that. And the question of when the diving might happen was a question now infrequently asked.

Captain Burke, the implacable taskmaster expected an all out effort from his crew as well as attentiveness from those in his navigation class, all in addition to their other shipboard duties. Quigley seemed satisfied, but whether their efforts met with the approval or otherwise of the captain, they had no way of knowing, his countenance remained the same, uncompromisingly stern. Never once did he pass a pleasantry or a salutation. Not once did an unnecessary word pass his lips. He would issue an order and expect it to be carried out and nothing more. Even so, the crew's attitudes were changing. The routine now seemed so normal to them that the trepidation they had felt on that first night disappeared. The work they were doing was hard but it was in no way incompatible with their interest in diving and there was an appropriate reason for every order, they could see that. And behind the labors there was always the sustaining reality that soon they would drop anchor over the Great Barrier Reef and start diving.

There was little time for Val to corner Tommy for their promised heart-to-heart discussion on their future together. But she seemed to be content to wait for the right moment—time spent together—for now, was enough. In fact, they became closer in a very different way than they had ever known. Val was happy and so was Tommy and both were becoming more in harmony with their current environment. More and more they were able to spend time together, perhaps not completely alone as she wanted but time together nevertheless, snuggling and embracing when the time and opportunity presented itself. On the deck in the moonlight or when like the others they were at rest and lounging around the main cabin. After all they were a couple and everyone of the crew was well aware of the fact. But they had not been able, as yet to make their way to the cabin that Val had found for them to spend time in ultimate privacy—but that would come.

The crew was not even close to being real sailors but there was no doubt they were not landlubbers anymore. They had learned more in those few days than they ever had a right to expect and in all hearts there beat a pride that went with hard work and accomplishment. There was just one thing left for them to do.

Climb to the top of the masthead. The mainmast, the highest point on the ship, and everyone had to do it. They stood in a line waiting for the order from the captain to start, Quigley stood by ready to send them up. They would take to the rope ladder in their turn. Jeff however, artfully threaded his way back nearer the end of the line. For all his machismo Jeff wasn't that keen on heights. Not afraid, it just wasn't his thing. It wasn't easy, all the way to the topmost spar at the masthead—up one side—down the other.

The captain nodded and Quigley gave the order. There were three or four of them that were absolutely eager to go. They took off from the front of the line and scampered up lickety-split, Tommy and Val and were right behind them, Spencer went next. Of the ones that followed, some were perhaps a little nervous but once they could see others going up and then down ahead of them they sucked it up and took off up the rope ladder. Jeff hung back as long as he could, shuffling back through the line, until there were only two of the girls behind him.

'Move it, jock.' Debbie told him.

'Yeah, get going muscles,' Laura said, 'you're holding up us real sailors.'

Making something of a show in doing so, both girls moved around and ahead of him. 'Come on Laura, this guy ain't going anywhere.'

'Right behind you,' Laura pushed past him.

Jeff was the only one left on this side of the deck, most of them had negotiated the trip and were down on the other side of the ship the remainder were on the way down. Finally Jeff started up the ladder. Surprisingly, he made his way up and reached the top as fast as the best of them and started down the other side. Feeling so much more confident with each step down the rope ladder that by the time he got to the middle yardarm, Jeff, being

Jeff, began to goof around. Leaning out and away from the mast, faking a fall and a lot of other mindlessness. The others began yelling at him, some for him to stop while others urged him on.

'Stop it and get down here!'

'Yo! Go Jeff!'

'Come on down!'

The catcalling and yelling only encouraged him to do more outrageous stunts. He locked his feet around the ropes and leaned his body outwards. The captain was taking note of all this and gave new steering orders to the helmsman, Sulkar.

'Bos'n,' he said softly. 'Let her run with the wind.'

'Aye, aye Sir.'

With the wind behind her the ship gained speed immediately.

'Hard to port Bos'n—hard over!'

Caught by the sudden maneuver Jeff was flung all the way out over the deck and beyond. A fast running green sea with breaking whitecaps was all he could see below him. It took all his considerable strength for him to grapple his ungainly way back to the relative safety of the mast and yardarm but that was only brief sanctuary. For now the captain ordered the ship turned even more so that the wind was driving the ship from the starboard quarter and caused her to lay over to a hazardous angle.

'Hold her right there!' Captain Burke called.

The ship heeled over so much that the scuppers began to run hard with sea water all the way along the port side of the middle deck. Jeff's position was so precarious now that he couldn't go up and he couldn't go down. He just held on tenaciously to whatever he could. Jeff looked greener by the second, so much so that those below were afraid he might pass out and be unable to hang on any longer. It was about that time that Jeff said bye-bye to breakfast.

The captain turned to the wheelhouse with another command. 'Ease your helm Bos'n.'

The ship righted herself and a now very white faced Jeff climbed down gingerly to a hearty welcome back on deck by his shipmates.

That night the Erehwon dropped anchor over the Great Barrier Reef.

Six

For the next three days the crew got what they had come for. Diving the Great Barrier Reef. It was to them, as it is to every diver who had done it before them, the experience of a lifetime. All duties were suspended, meals were taken whenever they liked, in groups, one or two at a time or grab something on the run and hurry back to the water. They could dive to their heart's content. And that's exactly what they did. No work just diving and more diving.

The *Erehwon* was anchored about three miles south of the Magnetic Passage and many miles off the nearest land, an Aboriginal settlement called Palm Island. Spencer had read all about it as he did with most other things. It was named by Captain Cook after the cabbage palms that grow there. It had low mountains, and sandy beaches fringed with coral reefs. Spencer told Tommy, that the Island was the home of many of the Aboriginal people, some of whom could date their families all the way back to the original inhabitants but for others, their forebears were forced there by the British in the late eighteenth century.

The ship rode easily on the anchor cable as the weather was nothing short of perfect. The sea was almost dead calm, except for a rolling ground swell that did nothing to detract from the most excellent of diving conditions. In fact the swell gave intriguing movement to the live reef. From the deck, when the incoming and outgoing tides turned the ship around, to afford them different views of the reef through the crystalline blue water. They were in diving rapture and electrified by the magnificence of the reef and its aquatic inhabitants. The beauty of the reef with its incredible variety of color along with the denizens of infinite variety was nothing short of breathtaking.

Diving in groups and never less than pairs they saw an infinite variety of sea creatures that from time to time included some of the most dangerous, barracuda, fang tooth, a dragon fish and a viper fish and one of the most frightening of all, the infamous and well-named coffin fish. And sharks. Spencer had read that the reef was home to one hundred and sixty species of shark alone. Along with hundreds of others of the more benign species. Spencer and his diving partner at the time, Wally were treated to a glimpse, as it went on its way, a vampire squid and seconds later, a lion fish. The hard work they had to endure to get them to this point was well worth it and was by now entirely overlooked, even appreciated. The water was gloriously warm so the swimmers, the girls in particular, in their very brief costumes, provided an enchanting addition to the overall beauty of the underwater setting and something that did not go unnoticed by the masculine members of the crew. And then there was the splendor of the Reef itself—color bursting with every imaginable hue from the dramatic reds and blues and even blacks to the more delicate greens and brown. The Reef—pulsating with unique aquatic life.

In the evenings, of the diving days, they relaxed around the deck. The air they breathed was beyond perfection, it seemed as though they were the only people to ever take in such a freshness that had with it, along with the smell of the sea, an unidentifiable fragrance that filled their lungs and gave them a sense of verve and delight. And in quietly gazing in wonder at the marine phosphorescence when a school of fish would swim by stirring the water alight with that intriguing effect.

'What causes that?' Wally wondered.

'Ask brain man.' Jeff told him.

'Okay, do you know what that's all about, Spencer?'

'Phosphorescence. It's chemical.'

'Chemical really? But I still don't get why it lights up like that?'

'It's like a heatless light generated by marine plants and animals, it's bioluminescence is exhibited by a wide variety of oceanic organisms, from bacteria to large squids and fish, the light itself is emitted when a flavin pigment called lucifein is oxidized in the presence of luciferase, the chemical system is like that of fireflies. However, most of the homogeneous phosphorescence of the sea, the glowing wakes and the like is caused by the presence of a blooming phytoplankton, most notably the microscopic dinoflagellate called, noctiluca millaris.'

'Is that all?' Jeff queried sarcastically.

'No, it also effects some types of jellyfish.'

The crew were, for the most part, pretty bright with well adjusted, inquisitive minds but some of them were a little taken aback at Spencer's ability to recount facts from his didactic memory. Not so much those who knew him well, but others, the Australians naturally, were impressed. That was not his intention. It never was. Spencer was not a show off. It was quite simply that he had the mental dexterity to retain accurately everything he had ever read, heard, seen or said. Spencer was already the recipient of an excellent education to this point, however, a lot of his knowledge came about because he wanted to know everything about, well, everything, and that, in actuality, excluded practically nothing. So, in addition to his formal education, that made him, somewhat autodidactic. He had such an elevated degree of varied interests of which few people, including most scholars, were capable. Scholars are customarily immersed in one particular subject. Not so Spencer who was interested in, and able to retain facts about almost anything. In every other respect he was a likable, all round, regular teenager.

As the evenings, shifted on into night, those that had the voice for it would sing. One of the Aussie's had a guitar, the only musical instrument on board unaffected by the battery taboo. Or they just quietly enjoyed the ambiance knowing that this was a once in a lifetime experience that they would remember forever. And they had fun with each other too. Siu Ming for instance, turned out to have a well tuned sense of humor, perhaps not as dry as the Englishman, Matthew but just as well honed. Siu Ming, on one of his trips down to the reef had taken a pair of sun glasses with enormous white rims down with him. He attached them to a large, slow moving lobster then he pointed it out to Laura. Most of the evening that followed, Laura tried to convince the others that she had really seen a lobster wearing sun glasses. But when she asked Siu Ming to back up her story of the laid back lobster, he wouldn't say yes but he didn't say no either. He simply responded by putting on the all-too-well-known Oriental enigmatic expression. But by doing it so way over the top—the gag was over.

Near the end of third day of diving the idyllic scene was winding down into the late afternoon, the light was beginning to fade, consequently with less sunlight filtering down, the water was becoming less clear. Most of them were pretty tired anyway. It was time to call it a day. They were about ready to swim to the surface when an ominous note was struck. Spencer and one of the others saw, or thought they saw, a large, strange sea creature, something, swim by very fast. It disappeared quickly between two groupings of tall coral. They only had a quick flash but it was enough to cause concern to show on the faces of Spencer and the other diver he was partnered with, Alex. Once out of the water most of them climbed the rope ladder to the deck of the Erehwon from the longboat laying alongside that had been lowered there to allow them easy access to the water. Spencer, Alex and a couple of the others stayed in the long boat for a few minutes talking.

'Did you see that? What was it, Spencer?'

'I didn't get a good look at it, just a shadow. It could have been a shark.'

'Grouper,' Tommy said, 'people say they get awful big around these waters, did it look like a grouper? Alex?'

'Gee, don't know, it was big though and, and sort of well, not fish like yet it had to be and—'

'Yeah?'

'And sort of well, different, you know?

'Just some big fish,' Tommy said, 'not unusual, there's a lot of fish down there, you know, could be anything.'

'Well, I know I saw something,' Alex insisted, 'something—'

'You said, big?' Tommy was curious.

'Yeah big, I guess, hell I don't know now, well yeah, big.'

'Grouper,' Tommy said, 'probably a grouper.'

'No, it was too quick, right Spencer?'

'It was fast,' Spencer agreed, 'too fast for grouper I think.'

'You lot down there,' Quigley called from the deck, 'come aboard, and stand by to hoist the long boat.'

The long boat was hauled aboard and secured back onto its place on top of the middle deck superstructure and covered. Quigley told them that there would be no more diving, that watches and the general work schedule would resume. This came at no surprise or disappointment. They had had plenty of diving for now. He also told them that all hands, everyone including those who had duties below, the cooks and galley hands were to stop what they were doing and muster on deck in the morning at eight bells.

'Hey, mister Quigley,' Jeff asked, 'how about giving the batteries back?'

'Batteries?'

'Yeah, our batteries.'

'Oh, batteries,' Quigley laughed, 'like I just said, all hands on deck at eight bells.'

'What's going on?' Tommy asked him.

'The captain don't whisper everything into my little ear, boy.'

'Yeah, but you know don't you?'

'You gotta be sharp on deck at them eight bells, that's all.'

With that Quigley went forward and the rest of them went below.

The next day shortly after the Bos'n had swung the bell rope eight times, two rings at a time, the crew were standing to on deck. They were a little boisterous but stood in a more or less straight line as they faced Quigley. Except for the good natured kidding there was no sound other than the gentle lapping of waves on the ship's side from an offshore breeze that was beginning to freshen. The captain, as usual, hardly noticed their arrival. He was positioned just outside the wheel house hatchway, his eyes fixed on the open sea. The crew gradually quietened down to the point that they were standing still and quiet.

Quigley saluted, fingers touching his cap smartly.

'All hands standin' to on deck, captain.' He said.

The captain didn't answer right away and his gaze only left the sea when at last he spoke.

'Very well.'

He walked slowly to the center of the deck, in front of the wheel house, and looked at the crew. It was a strange inspection. He saw them but it was as though they were not there at all—as though he was staring at an empty deck. Minutes passed then his gaze turned to the sea again. After what seemed to those waiting on deck, an interminably long time, he seemed to come to a decision and a moment later, nodded a silent command to Quigley.

'Off hats!' Quigley ordered removing his cap.

Those that were wearing caps, and that was most of them, generally baseball or peaked caps of one type or another, took them off following the order and Quigley's example. The captain did the same. There was a little shuffling and fidgeting by one or two and at the end of the line, Jeff playfully nudged the man on his right a number of times. Captain Burke turned cold eyes on Jeff and the others who quickly straightened up and stood still again. Not until there was absolute silence did the captain begin to speak. His words were spirited but not bellowed. Even so, his voice was heard clearly from one end of the deck to the other.

'Great master of the ocean,' he began, 'thou seest our weaknesses, and thou knowest our needs, grant that we may quit ourselves as men in the trials and dangers that lay before us. Protect us from the perils of the sea, watch over us, strengthen our hearts and in thy mercy and compassion bring us in safely to the haven toward which we now direct our course.'

'On hats!' Quigley ordered sharply.

'Mister Quigley!'

'Aye, sir.'

'Hoist anchor! Set main'sils and top'sil,' he bellowed, 'bos'un, man the helm!'

From that moment things began to happen quickly.

'All hands to your stations!' Quigley pointed at Tommy. 'You boy, go to the wheel house, do what the bos'un tells you.'

Quigley set them to work in gangs, those raising the anchor, or hauling on the rigging lines but for others, one or two for one job or another. It was not in any way analogous of that first time. They knew pretty much what was to be done and went about it fast but in an orderly manner. The training, short and intense though it was, was paying good dividends. They knew their stations now, what had to be done and they did it.

'Quick about it now! Bend to it sailors!' Male or female Quigley seemed to make no distinction, he called them all sailors, boys, lads or swabbies.

'Set main sail, jib and foresail jib!' Captain Burke called loudly.

'Jibs captain?' Quigley queried.

Quigley knew that it was a lot of sail even for experienced men, for a green crew it was an out-and-out challenge. At any time that much canvas would make the ship extra lively and perhaps difficult to handle.

'That was the order, Mister, jibs,' then he said, 'jibs, t'gallants and royals!'

'Aye, aye sir, jibs, t'gallants and royals it is.'

Quigley knew better than to do no more than confirm his captain's orders—never to question any command or reasons for them even though the order startled him.

White canvas sails, one after another were hauled up or dropped into position and began to fill with wind like great albatross' opening their wings to take to the air after a long spell of idleness on a flat sea. The *Erehwon* came awake and with the bow lifting slightly she began to move through the water.

'Bring her round, helmsman,' the captain called to the wheel house, 'set course, East by nor East.'

Sulkar swung the wheel gently to the right and held it there until the compass rose registered zero five zero then steadied the ship's wheel to amidships on that bearing.

'East by nor East! Captain,' he called, 'zero five zero.'

'Very well.'

When all the sails were set and taking a now stiffening breeze coming out of the west, it gave the crew the opportunity to feel the ship for the first time under enough canvas to make her cut through the water. Then the breeze quickened into gusts and in turn, to a really strong, steady blow. She was not running with the wind behind her so the westerly direction from which it came was heeling the ship on to her starboard side by several degrees. The bow dipped into and cut through the swell securely and rose again only to go down deeper and back up higher each time as the ship picked up more and more speed. The crew had not felt this motion before when sailing up and down the coastline as they had been doing under very light sail. But they were by no means apprehensive, in fact they were beginning to appreciate the ever increasing speed. Added to that was the knowledge that they were the people making it happen. A special feeling of rich awareness began to stir in them. They were sailing in a tall ship under a great deal of sail power—every inch of canvas the ship possessed.

Even after all sails had been set there was still a lot of work to be done, some eased or braced lines at Quigley's direction. Others had duties that were somewhat new to them but for the most part they now knew what they were doing. They began to, not only welcome what was happening, but thrill with enthusiasm, a huge buzz surged through everyone. Sulkar, at the helm, held the wheel over to the starboard side at an even pressure but now and again the ship would be pushed a little off her course and he would ease or add pressure to the helm to compensate and bring her back to the correct heading. That kind of handling took experience and practice before anyone could be called a true helmsman. Sulkar then did something unexpected. He turned the wheel over to a surprised Tommy.

'Look there,' he pointed, 'what is bearing?'

'Zero five zero,' Tommy answered as he took an uncertain and positively white knuckled grip on the wheel, 'east by north east.'

'Hold that, steady as she goes, say it?'

'Yes sir, steady as she goes.'

'Bos'n, you say bos'n, I not sir. Captain Sir, I bos'n, you say.

'Bos'un. Steady as she goes, bos'n.'

Just how much they had learned in such a short time was confirmed as the *Erehwon* turned her stern to the land and headed out. A sparkling sea complimented by the now strong off shore wind that had whipped up, as though by design, to see the ship on her way in the most splendid fashion. The glorious morning sunshine saw the old ship sailing magnificently almost abeam of the wind. The result of the labors of every hand aboard. Each at his or her appointed station began to understand what it meant to have pride in your ship as the *Erehwon* cut majestically through the waves and out into the deeper water of the great Pacific Ocean.

Faces on board seemed to radiant with that pride, together perhaps with the self-confidence that comes only with hard labors and personal achievement. Watching ahead to the Bowsprit and above to the highest part of the mast while mastering, and mastering quickly, moving around on the acute angle of the deck without stumbling or worse, and looking like a landlubber. Quigley moved over and stood at the lee side braces watching over his crew.

'She sure is going fast, Mister Quigley,' Alex called to him over the rushing sounds of wind and spray

'Fast? There's blue water under her keel boy—she's flying!'

'Yeah!' Alex shouted at the top of his lungs, *'she's flying! She's flying!'*

Some of them seemed to lean forward as if to give their own strength so that the gallant old ship might cut through the waves at an even greater pace. Not one of them had ever felt anything like it before. The ship, under full sail, main and fore sail, top sails, two jibs and royals and topgallants, was, as Quigley had said and Alex had shouted—'flying!' Flying over blue water to their amazement, excitement and consummate delight.

Those on the fore deck or on the windward side were constantly dashed in the face with heavy spray as the bow dipped low in the water and rose high above then plow deeper and rise higher than the one before. Then something strange caught the eye of Spencer and several of the others. Captain Burke suddenly became extremely aroused. He strode briskly to the starboard railing, raised an arm and pointed at the vast, empty ocean and called in a thunderous voice, *'To sea! To sea!'*

Seven

'Hey Cookie! More potatoes.'

The crew, for now they thought of themselves as a crew, were at the table for the evening meal. There was a lot of general noise with loud, excited talk and banter about the events of the day.

'Ask the mess hand, Frank,' Mary said leaning out of the galley, 'not the cooks or galley hands, the mess hand, Frank.'

'Oh, boy, protocol.'

'Amplification,' Spencer said, 'protocol and order stimulates efficiency.'

'Okay, so where's the efficient mess hand, yo! Mess hand more potatoes.'

'I got it.' Wally, on that duty, delivered another bowl of mashed potatoes to the table.

Quigley passed by the door on the other side of the galley. The first mate, for the most part, stayed out of their way when they were not on duty. He was unnoticed by most but Jeff spotted him.

'How come he doesn't eat with us?' Hooking his thumb at the galley.

'Who?'

'Quigley, how come he never eats here?'

'Who knows?' Jenny said.

'Who cares,' Laura added.

'Probably saw Jeff eating and it turned his stomach.' Debbie teased.

'Funny, funny.'

'They have a separate galley.' Spencer told them.

They talked nonstop about what it had been like, what each of them had done during what they were now calling, *'the wild ride'*. The flying sail that had gone on for six hours before the captain ordered the rig to be reduced to the mains and jibs and altered course accordingly to a take her on a more even balance of wind and rig. The ship responded well and began cutting more gently through the water rather than the deep up and down bow plowing motion of when she was traveling at high speed. Then the wind had softened to a breeze again and turned to a more northerly direction and the captain, by procedure or, perhaps rather than fight it by tacking back and forth, had changed course and trimmed down the sails with just half of the main sails and no jibs or top sails so that the ship made way a lot slower but more comfortably.

Six hours but what six hours. Not one of them had ever experienced anything like it in their lives. For more than thirty minutes Tommy was the man who had absolute control of the ship. After that some of the others were given the same chance. But most could not keep the ship on course for more than a few seconds at a time. Sulkar would move the temporary helmsman out of the way and get the ship back on course. After Tommy other members of the captain's navigation class were given a shot, Spencer followed by Val and so on. Then the rest of the others were given a shot at steering the ship for a few minutes then sent back to their duties. After which Tommy, Spencer, Jeff and Val were rotated for short periods. Tommy was by far the best helmsman but Spencer was pretty good and so was Jeff. They didn't feel any pressure and took on the job with enthusiasm especially Jeff. Whatever their job, whatever any of them did during that time, they did well. And now, in the evening, all were basking in the afterglow of their accomplishment and of the roller-coaster ride.

The next day there was practically nothing for them to do. They went through the watches of course but since the ship was moving at a leisurely pace over a slow rolling sea with no broken water it was smooth sailing. They took it easy. Quigley and Sulkar did all the steering, the captain was nowhere to be seen. Even though what had to be done was somewhat minimal they had without a doubt become more competent in their tasks so life aboard the *Erehwon* took on a fairly serene tempo. The weather was superb, they were reasonably comfortable in their quarters, they were well fed and among friends, what was not to like?

Later, a perfect night, found them relaxing quietly on or near the fore deck, the *Larrikin's Deck*. One of the Aussie's strummed lightly on the guitar. Val and Tommy, snuggled together, gazed at, and along with others, tried to identify the stars. The obligatory *Uranus* pun was quickly run off, unsurprisingly by Jeff.

Captain Burke was on deck just aft of the wheelhouse. He too looked up at the stars.

'Hanging out, captain?' Jim said as he was taking a turn about the deck as part of his watch.

'Hanging out?'

'Ah, nothing.'

The captain took another glance up at the stars and called to the man at the wheel.

'You're five degrees off, bos'un'

'Aye, captain.'

Sulkar turned the wheel a little to bring her back on course.

'You know, we can't see the coast anymore?' Beth said, 'I didn't see it at all today did you?'

'Yeah, but we're heading in a westerly direction now,' Tommy told her, 'probably see it tomorrow,'

'That is if we don't change course again.' Spencer reasoned.

'We're too far out to see any land,' Tommy figured, 'or maybe there was some sea mist, between us and the coast today.'

'I like to see the shore,' Laura said, 'it's sort of comforting.'

'I don't care,' Beth said, 'on a night like this, I don't care about anything.' Alex smiled and nodded his agreement.

'This is nice,' Val murmured as she nudged him lightly and snuggled in even closer contentedly. 'Except for *you know what*,' looking up into his eyes, 'you *do* know what, Tommy?'

'Of course, but we've had no time since we've been on the ship.'

'That's true my sweet, but we'll be able to find the time soon I think, we have to get things settled.'

'Are you sure there's no test you can do?'

'No test! Come on Tommy we just have to talk it out.'

'Maybe, but you know something? I'm about ready to end this trip, anyway, aren't you?'

'No! Not if it's all like tonight.'

'I get the feeling that it's not going to be—like it's—'

'What?'

He shrugged.

'Don't know, just a feeling.'

'At first I didn't want to take this trip,' Val said, 'remember?'

'Yeah, you didn't.'

'I was the one who was skeptical about taking the boat thing when we heard about it at that hotel.'

'Backpackers.'

'Okay, backpackers. We only came to Australia for a break and to see some of the country, but who knew it would be so wonderful—I mean the boat's not much but on nights like this, Tommy, could anything be better?'

'Nights like this, yeah Val, but good things can't last. We need to get back now anyway.'

Further along the deck they could hear some of the others talking.

'What about you, Alex?' Beth was saying, 'for me on a night like this I could go on forever.'

'Me too.'

The weather had become more active through the night and by dawn a fairly lively sea was running. It was not what could be called rough but it continued to roll the vessel on a side to side motion throughout the day. The ship was still heading to the west with the same minimum sail power so there was again, not a lot of work to be done and no calls for changes of sailing rig. They spent the day much as the one before except that the sea was breaking over the bow from time to time and there was more pitch and roll. Nothing to worry about really and none of the crew seemed to mind. Spirits remained high. That night was one of the few times that almost the entire crew ate at the same time. Loud, bright conversation filled the air, a lot laughs and a fair amount of kidding.

'Look,' Jeff said airily, I don't know and I don't care, okay?'

'Ignorance and apathy,' Jenny said, 'that's a hard combo to beat.'

'If you'll allow me Jeff,' Wally was about to try again, 'let me explain it to you, the way Quigley explained it to me.'

'Yeah Quigley, first name whackjob, okay shoot.'

'A boat is a vessel that you can put on a ship, got it?'

'No! They're both boats aren't they?'

'Well, not really, don't you get it?'

'I do.' Matthew said.

'Me too,' Siu Ming agreed, 'a ship can't be put on a boat, only visa versa, right?'

'Yeah,' Wally went on, 'if it's too big to be placed on another vessel, then it's a ship, that's the difference between a ship and a boat.'

'Okay, okay! I get it.'

'No he doesn't.' Beth cut in from the other side of the mess table.

'I do!'

Beth shook her head and put on a sad face.

'He doesn't, poor Jeff.'

'Shut the hell up!'

'Listen, Tommy listen!' Val said.

'What?'

There was still a noisy banter going on between Jeff and one or two of the others so Val held up both hands. 'Listen! Quiet everyone! Quiet!'

The joking and teasing trailed off until there was quiet.

'What is that?'

'Well, I can't hear anything and—' Jeff began but was interrupted by Val and some of others.

'Quiet!'

'Listen!'

It was not long before they could all hear it. A low doleful sound. Flute like in essence, but not really, perhaps more like a French horn, but again, not really. Hardly tuneful—certainly not music—but quite light in nature. Variable, and somewhat pitiful. None of them could say they had ever heard a sound like it before.

'What the hell is it?' Jeff said.

Now everyone at the table was listening. The sound changed a little. It became clearer and very slightly louder. And as it did so, the ship began to steady. The pitch and roll of the vessel started to subside and the sea leveled to calm until it became as smooth as silk. Until there was no sea motion at all. Not from the sea, not from the ship and absolutely not from those at the table. The usually swaying lanterns became as rigid as rocks.

No one moved.

'This is creepy.' Patty whispered very softly.

Then silence.

And even though her three words were barely audible it had a chilling effect on others around the table. The ship was now totally motionless as though she were set in granite. And the disturbing sound continued. For long minutes the ship was as though it were a mass of stone sitting in the middle of a silent desert. No wind, no waves, and no sound other than the mournful sound that seemed to, ever increasingly, lay a blanket of stillness over those at the table.

It lasted for some time then quite slowly the sound began to drain away to finally fade away. It was replaced by, at first, a soft wind then, the waves swelling and breaking at the side of the vessel. The ship took on life again.

Curiously, as the sound died out it left many of them with the feeling that it was still there but that they could no longer hear it. That was absurd, if it could no longer be heard it wasn't there. Yet, the feeling persisted. And not one of them could be sure how long it had lasted. And an odd feeling that they could not be certain when it had began and when it had ended. As though the episode had been a separate piece of time—an interruption—within the reality. The carefree atmosphere of the days before diminished and then completely disappeared. And for reasons they could not explain to themselves or each other.

Eight

'Alex. . . Alex!'

Tommy was among the several of those searching.

'Alex! Alex!'

He was about to open one of the hatches on the main deck superstructure when Spencer ran up to him.

'Find him?' Tommy asked.

'No sign of him.'

'Where's Quigley?'

'Wally went to get him.'

With Wally at his heals others now on deck, crowded around as Quigley joined them.

'Where have you looked?'

'He's not in the mess or the galley,' Val told him.

'Mister Quigley we've looked all over!' Wally told him.

'Below?' Quigley wanted to know.

'All around and the mess,' Wally answered, 'we can't find him.'

'You . . . ah,' Quigley said, 'keep looking . . . I'll go get the captain.'

'That will not be necessary, Mister.'

Turning, they could see the captain emerging from the hatchway at the side of the wheel house. Quigley went back to him. Tommy and some of the others followed.

'Report, Mister Quigley.'

'One of the lads, captain, he's missing.'

'Missing?'

'Aye, sir.'

'Very well,' the captain said quietly, 'Mister Quigley, you will organize a search of the ship.'

'I told Mister Quigley,' Wally said, 'we've looked—'

Captain Burke ignored him and turned away.

'Search, the ship.' He repeated.

'Aye, aye.'

Quigley went into action.

'All hands! split up into groups, here, you three go forward, you lot go aft, you come with me, the rest of you go below, start from the aft companionway back to the bulkhead and go forward, galley, sleeping quarters, the forward cabins, lockers, go!'

'Hey! We've looked there already!' Jeff told him.

'Do it again, now!' Quigley said pointing to Tommy and Spencer, 'you two stay by the captain and wait on his orders.'

They ran off as Quigley had directed, Tommy and Spencer stood by, near the captain who pursed his lips a little and his eyes made a sweep of the ocean but otherwise gave no sign to tell them if he shared their concern or not.

'Who is it?' He asked them without turning his gaze away from the sea, 'what name?'

'Alex,' replied Tommy, 'he was on the aft deck watch from four to eight o'clock,'

'Eight bells.' The captain corrected him.

'Eight bells. When Jim went to relieve him he found no one there.'

'And the forward watch?'

'Wally was on forward watch,' Spencer told him, 'he said he came back a few times during the watch and Wally said he was there then.'

'Send for him.'

Spencer ran off to get Wally. The rest of the crew, one after another, began reappearing on deck. In another minute Wally stood before the captain.

'You were on the forward watch?'

'Yes sir.'

'When was the last time you saw him?'

'About an hour before the watch ended.'

'Hmmm, two hours ago,' Captain Burke said as he shielded his eyes and squinted up at the sun, 'report Mister Quigley.'

'Not on board, sir.'

'Very well,' he said. Then after thinking for a moment, 'all hands to stations, Mister Quigley, stand by to put about.'

'Aye, aye, sir,' Quigley reacted, 'go to your stations and stand by to go about.'

The captain went toward the wheelhouse as they hurried away to their places.

'Port helm — hard over.' He told Sulkar. After the ship had made a tight hundred eighty degree turn he went up to the wheel. 'Go forward, Bos'n, I'll take the helm.'

Later, almost the whole crew, those who didn't have to stand by their stations, were up forward on the highest part of the upper deck, probing the sea. Jeff and two of the others, without orders to do so, climbed up into the rigging for a better view. There was no crow's nest on the ship so he positioned himself just under the first spar. Spencer came to the bow where Tommy and the rest of them were searching the sea for any sign of Alex.

'Tommy,' Spencer said, 'Quigley says this would be about the place where he would have fallen overboard.'

'Who says he fell overboard!' Beth said heatedly as tears began, 'maybe he didn't,' Val put a comforting arm around Beth as her voice trailed off, 'maybe he's still on the boat.'

'Ship.' Someone said thoughtlessly.

'Screw you!' Beth exploded, 'ship boat I don't give a shit! We have to find him!'

'Keep looking,' Tommy said. 'Everyone keep looking.'

Hours later they were pretty much in the same positions. Lucent sunshine spread over an ocean that had with it not a serious wave in sight. They would have been able to see the smallest object on the surface for miles had there been anything. The only clouds to be seen were some twenty miles away to the north, they could see to the far horizon in every direction. From time to time others would take the places of those in the rigging only Jeff stayed up there. Most of them were searching from near the bow feeling sure that there would be the best place to spot any sign of Alex. The somber mood of the crew inevitably meant that there was little talk. Nobody wanted to say anything that might disturb them more that they already were if that were even possible.

The ship had made a circular course since returning to the location that Captain Burke had indicated as the place most likely to recover the lost crewman. Four times complete three hundred and sixty degree circles had been made and with each circle the captain had effected the adjustment for the tides so the circles had moved to the south, overlapping each by half with each loop. Quigley and the bos'un used their keen eyes and experience in the search also but, to no avail. Alex was not found. Quigley, returning from the wheel house, stood quietly behind them on the fore deck for a moment before speaking.

'Captain wants all hands aft.'

Nobody moved.

'Come on Val,' Tommy said taking her by the hand. They started back toward the aft end of the ship with the others following slowly behind making their way to the middle deck to where the captain was standing in front of the wheelhouse. They bunched up at that point and waited. Captain Burke watched them carefully before he said anything.

'Ships company,' he began in a low voice, 'I have made the following entry in the ship's log, Alex Martin,' he read from the log, 'a valued member of the crew of this vessel, while doing his duty in the service of the ship was this day lost to the sea.'

The shock of the loss of Alex had a terrible effect on them. So much so that there was little or no reaction to the captains words other than the sound of crying from some of the women. The men too were not immune to the powerful emotion of awful loss.

The captain waited for a moment before continuing.

'Mister Quigley.'

'Aye?'

'Resume the last course given.'

Those who were not on watch spent a restless night. But all of them, on watch or not, were now thinking about what had happened—what might happen—and recalling the time when they left home . . .

'Brisbane, Townsville, Cape Upstart or anywhere close!'

As a car approached they waved the sign and jerked their thumbs but the car flashed by at high speed leaving them in a cloud of country road dust. 'Come on mate, give us a break,' Frank smiled and turned to check for another prospect, 'bugger, he looked like he was going to stop.'

'We're never gonna make it.' Jack sighed.

'Sure,' Frank said confidently 'we'll make it all right.'

The two friends decided to rest on the roadside sitting on the duffel bags that were mostly stuffed with their diving gear.

'Cripes!' Jack said shaking his head, 'three days and we've still got a long way to go.'

'You know how far we've come, I mean from when we started?'

'No, seems like all of Aussie.' Jack shook his head again.

'Four hundred miles, that's bloody good, mate! Yeah, for sure, we'll make it, no worries.'

'But Frank—'

'No buts, we'll get there, no worries.'

Jack stared dejectedly at the road then let his head drop.

Frank put his arm around his friend's shoulder. 'We'll make it, mate.'

'We're on our way—bye-bye Kalgoorlie—hello Great Barrier Reef!' Wally yelled. 'We're actually going to the Reef!'

Along with two friends, Jim and Beth they were traveling east and later, north to Merinda and Cape Upstart.

'How far is it, again?' Beth wanted to know

'Forever.' Jim said.

'Does it matter?'

'Nope, a lot though,' Wally told them, 'oh, I reckon it's going to take us about thirty hours altogether.'

'And we have to change buses a couple of times, Beth.'

'Who cares—we're going to the Reef!'

'You know,' Jim cut in, 'we've got to be sure the gear gets transferred, you know to the next bus.'

'No worries mate!' Wally assured him, 'I'm going to do it myself.'

'Bye!

'Have fun!'

'You bet we will!'

The train was about to pull out of the cavernous Melbourne Central Railway Station with Kim, Patty and Karen aboard waving and shouting good-byes. The train began to pick up speed and soon disappeared.

Half way up Mount Victoria, the twenty five story Woodland Heights on Wongneichong Gap Road, the most fashionable part of Hong Kong. In one of the elegant condominiums that look out over the harbor to Kowloon and the New Territories a family sat at the table. The parents and their five children seated from the youngest, a little girl nearest to her mother, to the oldest. Siu Ming faced his father. They spoke in the Cantonese dialect.

'As first son you are aware that you have obligations to the family?'

'Yes, father.'

'Very well then,' his father said quietly, 'We will pray for your safe journeys and happy return to us.'

'Thank you father.' Siu Ming said respectfully.

'I'd better go now, Mother.'

The smartly dressed young man sat in the first class departure lounge of British Airways at London's Heathrow Airport with his two nervous parents.

'Oh, Matthew you will be careful won't you?'

'Of course, don't worry.' A smile meant to reassure his anxious mother.

'And you will keep in touch, promise?'

'It's a boat, we'll be at sea, don't fuss, mother. I'm not sure about the ports and all that.'

Matthew was tiring of the drawn out goodbye but he was, as he always was faultlessly polite when he expressed what he hoped would be the last of the requisite reassurances.

'Are you sure you have enough money, do you have your credit cards?'

'Oh, more than enough, thanks. I had better be going. Please don't worry mother, I'm sure they'll take good care of us. Well, good bye.'

He allowed her to kiss him on the cheek. His father shook his hand stiffly and he went on through the departure gate without looking back.

'How long will it take us to get there?' Laura couldn't keep the excitement out of her voice.

'Ask Spencer, he's the numbers guy.' Jenny turned Laura around to face Spencer.

Los Angeles Airport, usually crowded, hurried, and on occasion, chaotic, that night it was just busy. The Airliner standing at gate thirty seven proudly displayed the distinctive red kangaroo emblem on the tail and Qantas International Airlines emblazoned along the fuselage. In the departure area passengers waited for the boarding call. They were perhaps more eager than most of the other passengers especially those jaded by innumerable long, frequently monotonous plane rides. But the prospect of flying to Australia, on other side of the world was pretty heady stuff for this group.

'Okay, numbers guy, how long?'

'This flight,' he said pointing to the first page of a meticulously prepared itinerary, 'is a just over fourteen hours, we arrive at—'

'Fourteen hours?' Jeff grouched.

'We arrive in Sydney at eight thirty a m, Friday then—'

'Hey! This is Wednesday, what happened to Thursday?'

'We lose Thursday, Jeff, crossing the International date line we lose a day, but pick up a day coming back—there's a change of planes at Sydney, we catch one to Townsville via Brisbane and . . .'

'Another plane?'

'Yes, but only a couple of hours,' Spencer pivoted and looked up at Jeff who was several years older and five inches taller, 'didn't you read the itinerary I gave you?'

Jeff shrugged.

'Then, a bus ride to, see here,' Spencer flipped the pages, 'onto our final destination, a place called Cape Upstart.'

'Good evening ladies and gentlemen,' a welcoming voice came over the loud speakers, 'at this time Qantas International Airlines flight Zero one two, non stop to Sydney is now ready for boarding, please have your boarding passes ready and proceed to—'

They stood and moved quickly taking their places in line with other passengers.

'Cape Upstart.' Laura whispered dramatically.

'That's the place where we get on the boat.'

'Cape Upstart,' Jeff muttered, 'sounds—'

'Romantic,' Jenny enthused, 'Cape Upstart—sounds—*so romantic.*'

'Then,' Spencer folded the pages into his perfectly organized travel bag, 'on out to the Great Barrier Reef.'

'Can you believe it, Laura? Australia!'

'I know,' Laura shouted back excitedly, 'who ever thought we'd be diving the Great Barrier Reef? Australia here I come!'

'Jeff's just trying to be cool.'

'The diving, sure, the plane ride,' Jeff yawned, 'wake me when we get there.'

There was the usual bunching up the nearer they got to the plane door where the flight attendants were directing people to their seats. They were in the last rows of the economy section and were, of course, a little rowdy but not out of hand. Seasoned travelers seated nearby knew that the altitude would soon get to them and they would settle down and they did, talking more quietly to the one in the next seat and the row behind or in front.

'Oh Mary, what a great camera, must have cost a fortune?'

'It did, but it's worth it Laura, buy the best or buy nothing, my that's what my father says.'

'What's it like having a reverend for a father, I mean isn't he awful strict?'

'Minister, he's a minister, Laura,' Mary said, 'and he's no stricter than any one else.'

Jenny leaned in close to Laura. 'Well, you know everyone, all the stuff, Jeff for instance?'

'He's as dumb as dirt.'

'Just checking.'

'Well, I guess he's not dumb but he's no genius either,' Jenny told her. 'Hey, he's a jock.'

'Has he got a steady? He's kind of cute'

'I don't know, he's okay I guess.'

'You're going to get some great pictures,' Spencer observed, 'take a look at these brochures.'

'How come the Virgin Mary got to make the trip? Jeff asked Tony, 'I guess her old man loosened up.'

'She's a pretty good diver, better than most,' Tony told him, 'how about Fisher I thought he was on the trip?'

'Hey man, it's gotta be a better without that dork.'

'I thought he was okay.'

'Naw! He's a dork.

'Jeff, why are you always so angry,' Jenny said leaning across the aisle, 'so hostile?'

'A dork.'

Jenny said turned and faced the other way. 'Two carry on bags, Debbie?'

'Provisions, in case they don't have a good commissary on the boat.' 'Provisions huh?' Jeff said, 'I bet I know what you have in there, candy and chocolate, right?'

'So what, jock geek, what's in your bag, dumbbells?'

'You should get yourself in shape.' Jeff fired back.

Debbie was more sensitive about her slight chunkiness than most people realized. Not to say she was fat, far from it, just *a* size or so more than her trim companions. But there was no real venom in her voice when she said, only a little under her breath. 'Asshole.'

Late into the flight the lights had been dimmed, a movie was running but most of them were asleep, fatigue had finally overruled excitement. Debbie was awake—absorbed in the movie—munching on complimentary nibbles.

Nine

At sea, time passes in a different way to that of the land, there is no logical explanation for this phenomenon it just seems to happen. And it is different for different people, for some time seems to go by quickly while for others, it drags. And perhaps for that inexplicable reason, the loss of their friend Alex was unintentionally allowed to slip into the background. Of course some of them still talked about what happened and a few, those who knew him best, were still trying to get over it. And there was one other thing that was creeping some of them out. The impenetrably enigmatic Glorianna would be seen late at night slinking around different parts of the ship. More often than not garbed in some kind of dark colored caftan and with the heavy black makeup around her glaring eyes, inadvertently running into her in the darkness was enough to scare any of them out of their wits. When approached or spoken to she would offer what was presumed to be her version of a smile and quickly move away.

A life was lost. But life goes on and in that respect life itself had to be considered, many were starting to worry about their own safety. They were now talking to each other about getting back on to dry land and how soon that was going to happen. When they had broached the subject to Quigley, there being no question of bringing it to the captain, he had mumbled and walked away.

Concern was growing. In addition to that, the captain abruptly increased the workload. He found things for Quigley to tell them to do. They pretty much figured it was by design to keep them busy, so as not to dwell on the death of their friend if they were kept occupied they would not have time to think about Alex. To a significant extent that is just what happened.

Another thing that had changed, it seemed as though now Captain Burke treated them as though they were ship's property. As though the crew was signed on and not a group of vacation slash workers supposedly on board for a holiday slash dive cruise with a few ship-board duties. Most of them had the feeling that he considered them as simply the crew. When were they going to return to Cape Upstart? was the question—unasked for the most part, but certainly on everyone's mind. Resentment was natural but the situation demanded that they say and do nothing about it—for the time being.

'What the hell is that?'

Two days after Alex had disappeared they finished the evening meal, which was late that night so many of them were still sitting around the table.

'There it is again,' Jenny said, 'can't you smell it, Tommy?'

'Oh, yeah.'

'Last night too.' Wally affirmed.

'I didn't smell it last might,' Matthew told them, 'but I can now.'

'What a stink, yuk!' Debbie screwed up her face.

'A real pong, Wally said, 'even on deck you can smell it.'

'I can't,' Laura said, wheezing a little, 'I have the sniffles.'

'You're lucky, it's making me sick,' Jenny told her, 'well, I mean, you know last night and now.'

'It was stronger last night.' Siu Ming thought.

'No, it's worse this time.'

'Yeah, Spencer, what do you suppose it is?'

'Okay, who did it then, who cut one off?'

'Oh Jeff, you are so gross!' Mary rebuked, 'you know that, you're totally gross.'

'Spencer?'

'Hmmm, maybe it's,' Spencer replied thoughtfully, 'maybe—'

'Yes?'

He wavered.

'I don't know.' Spencer said at last. 'It's a mystery.'

The evening dwindled down in the mess cabin until they, one after another, drifted into the sleeping quarters and their bunks for a mostly restless night.

'What?' Tommy stared at Spencer.

'Jenny is missing, come on.'

Tommy's didn't want to be one of those individuals that people turned to in any kind of emergency and that's what he had told Val. Nevertheless, he had almost everyone paired up and scouring the ship within minutes. How could they all, himself included, have been so careless as to leave Jenny alone when one person had already gone missing? Soon everyone that was not on watch was searching the ship in much the same way as when Alex had first turned up missing. In ones and twos they went off in different directions.

'I'll go get Quigley?' Frank called as he turned to run on up the stairs that would take him to the deck.

'Not yet!' Tommy called him back, 'wait till we've looked down here.'

Tommy and those with him moved from aft to forward, while Spencer and some of the others moved along from forward to aft getting closer to each other all the time.

Wally waylaid Tommy and Val.

'Here, come with me, this way.' Wally said softly, placing a finger to his lips. They followed him to the door of one of the tiny forward cabins that Val had told Tommy about. Wally had them listen at the closed door for a moment, and then he opened it silently. By that time others had arrived and crowded around the doorway. There were two people in the bunk. Jenny tried to hide under a blanket as Jeff bellowed his annoyance.

'Fuck off!—asshole!'

Tommy closed the door and he, Val and Spencer walked back to the main cabin as the others dispersed. Wally went on up to the deck probably to inform those not already in the know of the incongruous twosome in the cabin.

'You want to hear something funny?' Spencer said.

'Please, Spencer pullessse!' Val said, 'tell me something funny, nothing is funny anymore, anything, tell us something that's funny.'

'Nobody missed Jeff.'

'You know, you're right,' Tommy said, 'nobody missed Jeff.'

'How about that, hmmm,' Val paraphrased, 'forgotten but not gone.'

They walked back toward the main cabin. Val pulled Tommy to a stop for a private word.

'I suppose you guessed it?'

'What?'

'That was the cabin I had in mind for us to be able to be alone, well shit!'

'But Val, there are other little places up there and—'

'Oh, I don't think so, not with everyone looking out for everyone else, and that's what we are doing isn't it?'

'We have to, till we get off this thing, don't we?'

'We do.'

'How are you, Spencer?'

'Is that a rhetorical question, Tommy?' Spencer did not immediately look up from the paper work on his desk when Tommy walked in, 'or do you really want to know? I'm going to assume that it is conversational and therefore rhetorical requiring no serious response, is that right?'

'Right. So how are you?'

'Conversationally, fine.'

He stacked books one on top of another and turned to face Tommy.

'I wanted to see you.'

'Yeah, Val told me, what's up?'

'Well, as you know, I, as ship's clerk have a lot of duties, including, making up the watch rosters, records of food for the galley from the pantry and keeping all manner of other registers necessary for the smooth running of a vessel at sea,'

'And becoming predictably efficient,'

'That is correct,' Spencer agreed without any of the false modesty many would affect, 'I also run the entire paper work of the ship, with the exception of the ship's log, that being the absolute prerogative of the Captain.'

'I'm kind of hoping there's a point to all this? If you're looking for a promotion, sorry, I can't give you one.'

Ignoring the remark, Spencer continued.

'In my spare time, I read.'

'No kidding?' Tommy's eyes widened in fake incredulity. 'You read!'

Again, Spencer ignored the light jibe.

'A lot of the stuff that's available on board, like The Seaman's Manual and Celestial Navigation to Jane's World Registry of Ships.'

'Okay, so?'

'So. . .'

'At last.'

'So, one of the books that I read here,' Spencer held a volume, 'Litanies of the Sea.'

'Again, so?'

'Remember when the captain said that entreaty or whatever it was? Well, he finished it with, quoting now, 'and bring us in safely to the haven toward which we now direct our course,' right?'

'Something like that?' Tommy said.

'Not something like that, exactly that, well I thought it sounded familiar but not quite right, naturally I looked it up,'

'Naturally,'

'And here is the exact wording,' Spencer read from the book, 'it says, bring us all in safely' do you see? All, he left out the word—*all!*'

'A mistake.' Tommy shrugged.

'He doesn't make mistakes.' Spencer argued.

'Then you did.'

'I don't make mistakes either.'

'Anyway, so what?'

'Don't you see? I don't think he means to bring us *all* in safely!' Spencer said, again emphasizing the word.

'A mistake Spence, his or yours it doesn't matter, just forget it.'

'I told you he doesn't make mistakes and neither do I,'

'Okay, even if both you and the captain are infallible—and nobody is, so what? Forget it Spencer,'

'I won't but, how about the name of this ship, *Erehwon*, right?' Spencer had something else on his mind.

'That's no mistake, *Erehwon*, what about it?' Tommy shrugged again.

At that moment Matthew stopped by, munching an apple.

'Gentlemen, what's up?'

'Definitely rhetorical.' Tommy observed.

'Later.' Spencer said as he closed the curtain.

'What's with him?' Jeff said as he and Val joined them.

Val placed her arm on Tommy's shoulder.

'Well?' She asked.

'Nothing.' Tommy said, taking her by the arm and walking them both into the main cabin, 'You know, things might be returning to normal.'

'Normal?' Val laughed. But it was not the kind of laugh that was bought about by something amusing. 'You mean what passes for normal on board a boat run by an iron-fisted captain and an anomalous first mate and God knows what the hell Sulkar is!'

'Anomalous first mate, Val, anomalous?'

'I didn't want to use the word abnormal, let's just say strange.'

'Whacko is fine with me.' Jeff said, 'and how the rest of us?'

Tommy could see that Val might be getting a little heated. A few of the others listened and some took seats around the table.

Spencer stood by the entrance at the other end of the cabin near the library shelves as he replaced the book he had shown Tommy as Val continued.

'Oh yes us, the crew!' Val turned to face Jeff. At the same time she reached for Tommy's hand which she took and held tightly in her own. 'A boat crewed by a bunch of land people, oh yeah, we may think we're sailors but we're just fooling ourselves, we don't know jack-shit about the sea and the ways of it.' Her eyes flashed at those either sitting or standing around the table, Mary and another girl poked their heads in from the galley to hear what was going on, they listened as Val continued.

'Don't any of you get it? We're like a bunch of morons doing what we're told to do, they've made us fall into such a routine that we have accepted Alex drowning as just one of those things, why, most of us don't even think of him anymore and it's only been a few days since it happened.' She wouldn't cry and didn't want to but tears of anger seemed like they were not far away. 'That's us all right, Jeff,' she said turning again to him, 'the poor Goddamned crew!'

Tommy put his arm around her. He knew better than anyone that this was not the self-confident and balanced Val that he knew so well. Val was smart and alert and always in control of her emotions. He had paid as much attention to her little speech as anyone but was at the same time, still thinking of what Spencer had said and why the brightest of them all had not wanted anyone else to know what they had been talking about.

The next day the ship labored sluggishly on a northerly course driven by a limp breeze under a paltry mainsail. The sun beat down on them with a grim torridness. It was the hottest day so far. There were only three of them that had any kind of duty, two on watch, one for and one aft and Tommy in the wheel house. He was steering the ship under very little supervision, Quigley was there for that purpose but he went out several times for one reason or another leaving Tommy alone in the wheel house. Tommy felt comfortable and confident, the ship was barely under way and he knew he only had to call the first mate at any sign of difficulty. The rest of them were for the most part just lounging around the deck, there was no organized activity. The workload had been inexplicably reduced again to practically nothing. Spencer, his duties taken care of, was relaxing on deck too, unsurprisingly a book of some kind close at hand. Mary and Laura sat talking on a part of the main superstructure just aft in the middle deck. Jeff and Wally were watching from a short distance away on the fore deck, the Larrikins deck.

'Gee, you don't take many pictures for a camera nut.'

'Enthusiast Laura, enthusiast. No I don't because I'm selective, what I take must be interesting and as near as possible to perfect.'

'They're just pictures.'

'Whenever anyone in my family goes on vacation we always make sure to take interesting pictures then we all sit down in the living room and that person runs them for the family on a big screen.'

'That stuff can be awfully boring.'

'Not our pictures, we always watch them together so it's exciting for the photographer as well.'

'Don't you look at them first?'

'Laura, that would take all the excitement out wouldn't it?'

'I guess so.'

Jeff had been miming some of the girl's conversation ending it by putting his finger under his nose and pushing it upwards indicating Mary's pretentiousness. He called to her and at the same time struck a muscular pose.

'Hey Mary, take my picture for the reverend and Mrs. Reverend?'

'Minister, he's a minister! no thanks, I don't want my parents going into shock,' she replied in the refined manner that had so far failed to put Jeff in his place, turning to Laura she said, 'he's such an idiot.'

Mary had Laura pose by some rigging and took her picture then Laura did the same with Mary a few steps up the rope ladder.

'Ugly board, u-g-o-l-y.' Jeff muttered under his breath.

'You kidding? She's an eight,' Wally told him what he thought, 'definitely an eight.'

'Not on my scale,' Jeff scoffed, his voice rising 'now you take a look at that Aussie chick, Kim, she is something man, that bikini is the size of a forty cent stamp, dude, that's a hot bod!'

'You know we can hear you, Jeff,' Mary called to him.

'So?'

'The body is the temple of the spirit.' Mary said piously.

'Is that so,' Jeff said nudging Wally in the ribs, 'well, in that case Kim is built like a brick temple,'

'A brick temple, huh.' Wally chortled.

Mary placed the camera on the superstructure and the two girls moved along the deck a little further and sat down there. Mary began showing Laura a few pictures in a small album. While they were thus occupied, Jeff crept up and took Mary's camera and went back to Wally.

'Now these were taken at Seminole National Park.' Mary said.

While up on the higher deck Jeff undid his belt and let the shorts drop around his ankles and bent over.

'Isn't that lovely?' Mary enthused—pointing to one of the pictures in the album.

Wally snapped a shot of Jeff's backside.

'Oh, dear, these are all mixed up, this one is of the Grand Canyon.' Mary said.

The glaring whiteness of Jeff's buttocks stood out against the deep tan of the rest of his body as Wally snapped off one more shot for good measure. Then Jeff turned around to face the camera. Wally suppressed a laugh as he clicked off another frontal shot.

'Here's a good one.' Mary said.

'Oh, that's a beauty!'

Jeff quickly slipped back into the shorts and crept up behind the girls to replace the camera in the spot where Mary had left it. He backed away, to join Wally. Jeff threw his head back in a silent laugh as they disappeared down the hatchway.

'Hey,' Val said turning to Spencer sitting nearby, 'did you see that?'

'No, what?'

Val told him. Spencer nodded.

'I guess they're just trying to have some fun, there's not much of that going around now,'

'I guess,' Val said, 'but it's kind of a mean trick, her father's minister, what are they going to think when they see Jeff's bare ass and accouterments?'

'It's mean all right,' Spencer agreed, 'I think I like it.'

'Okay, me too, a little.'

Ten

They crowded the main cabin later but there was much less high-spirited chatter than before Alex's disappearance, it was not the carefree ambiance of before perhaps but spirits were rising. The evening meal had just begun when they heard it. And again, at first there was the noticeable decrease in the pitch and roll to the ship. Inevitably, they looked at the lamps in their usually constant swing. The ship began to steady slowly, just as the time before, until there was very little motion.

Then they began to hear it. The less than tuneful notes of the mournful instrument became apparent to them as, one by one, they became aware that the baleful sound was back with them once more. The ship steadied. The sea became agonizingly calm, the lamps stopped swaying in the overheads and the water in their glasses stilled as though it had turned to ice. The lanterns beamed down on them casting shadows of fear filled uniformity. There was absolutely no movement whatsoever.

The Erehwon lay dead in the water. There was absolute silence. Then Beth let go with a kind of cry. It was not loud in fact it was quite soft more a whimper than a scream. But it had a terrible effect on some of them and caused them to do things quite out of character. Jenny took a strong grip on Matthew's arm and held on tightly. Others did similar things, as though the touch of another person offered security of some kind.

A feeling of vulnerability and fear began to take hold of them. After those emotions came, panic. All at once several of them jumped away from the table to run, but run to where? There was one or two sob-like sounds and those more spooked began to shout at one another. Beth's cry had perhaps expressed what many of them were feeling deep down even though it was not expressed in words it had a clear meaning. And it had been so unexpected and so startling that it alarmed several of them to the point where some were about to lose control altogether. And the uproar became more and more intense.

'Quiet!' Tommy yelled, 'get hold of yourselves!'

The commotion quieted down a little.

'Quiet, calm down!' Tommy called while holding out his hands motioning palms downwards a few times trying to drop the tension in the cabin. 'That's better,' he continued quietly, 'we have to keep calm and—'

'Someone's going to die tonight.' Tony whispered.'

'You shut your goddamned mouth!' Jeff shouted at him and the general clamor began all over again.

'You shut up, asshole!' Tony shouted back at him. Jeff was on his feet and ready to throw punches but Tommy stopped him.

'All of you shut up!' Tommy yelled above the noise, 'stop it, cool out, will you?'

'Please! Val called in a loud voice. She had, although inwardly just as shaken as the others, remained relatively composed during the hubbub and now joined Tommy in trying to suppress the rising panic by attempting to carry on as normally as possible. She had some help from one or two others and there was quiet again for the moment—it didn't last—the yelling started again.

'Please!' Val shouted, 'please!' They stopped and looked at her. Val's voice softened, 'please, would some one pass me the salad bowl?'

They were quiet for a moment looking at her in disbelief.

'What are you all nuts? Jenny yelled, 'can't you see what's happening!'

'You mean, what's going to happen.' Tony said.

Val remained as calm as she could, glancing around the table before speaking again.

'Nobody's going to die, Tony.' She said softly. 'That kind of talk will only upset people, let's try to be positive.'

A somewhat chastened, Tony passed her the salad bowl.

The doleful notes faded and the dead calm died away and the ship had motion again as slight waves washed comfortingly along the sides of the ship. The sea remained relatively inactive for the rest of the night. After the meal, which many of them had been too shaken to eat with any of the gusto that had become rather customary, Tommy, Val and Spencer went up on deck to see if they could find the source of the discomforting sound. They had no real idea of what to they were actually looking for and of course found nothing. The sound was gone and there was no indication what it was or where it had originated.

No stars could be seen that night. The sky had turned cloudy and murky, a lusterless moon found heavy clouds to hide behind and Val shivered even though the night was warm. Loose shrouds rattled lightly against the masts and even though they had become accustomed to the sound, in the blanket of darkness it had the power to unnerve them. Others came up from below. It was an eerie atmosphere in the black stillness surrounding the ship that was more than merely disturbing. Those that did not have the watch were not anxious to stay on deck for long. One after another they went below trying to find solace in the more conversant surroundings of the main cabin.

Here she was a completely normal, rational, educated and sophisticated young woman happy to be abandoning herself to her perfect lover in this tiny cabin. His touch alone was enough to bring her to a sensual height that she could never before have imagined and when he made love to her—she made love to him, holding nothing back. Love making that bought with it, for her, the ultimate in sexual gratification. He was forceful yet gentle, an oxymoron surely—yet—that was her man.

Their lips parted but they continued to hold each other tightly. For a few minutes they said nothing. Rather they luxuriated in the pleasure and assurance of what they had experienced before, the ultimate expression of their love for each other. He was her first and only real love and she, his. Yes, each of them had been involved in other relationships but looking back both Tommy and Val had before long come to the realization that those relationships had meant little—just something that everyone goes though until they find the right person. Val knew that this was the real thing, the only question on Val's mind was: would it last, could it be constant, could it be sustained? Tommy knew he loved Val but he was more blasé in his love—it was what it was—and he was relaxed with it. Val stroked his cheek, her eyes opened and she kissed him lightly on the lips and he kissed her only a little less gently. Tommy thought they were committed to each other and that was enough, Val needed to go deeper. But the things that had happened and might happen was now their minds.

'Tommy, I'm scared.' Val breathed softly.

Tommy had found another cabin further toward the bow that was to be their hiding place. Tommy had told Spencer that if they were to be thought missing he knew they were safe and just wanted some alone time.

'No one will find us in here.'

'I don't mean that, I'm scared of what's been happening, what might happen.'

'I know,' Tommy admitted, 'I am too, more than I want the others to know.'

'That's good, some of them look to you for strength.'

'Bullshit.'

'Yes they do. I know I do.' Val snuggled up placing a leg across his body her eyes fixed on his face. 'Tommy?'

'Yes.'

'Instead of on a boat, okay, ship, what would we be doing?'

'Sightseeing, I guess.'

Val nuzzled her head into his shoulder and smiled contentedly.

'Val, are you sorry we got on this trip?'

'Of course I'm sorry, aren't you?'

'I don't know,' Tommy said thoughtfully.

'Tommy, if Alex hadn't come on this ship he'd still be alive.'

'Oh, I guess so, but who can tell, maybe he was going to die anyway.'

'I don't believe that for a minute,'

'Who knows, maybe it was his time, his karma, his fate, you know.'

'That's just so much baloney!' she said lifting her head so as to look into his eyes, 'and you don't believe any of it, do you?'

'I guess not. Oh shit,' Tommy sighed, 'I don't know what I believe anymore.'

Val put her head back on his shoulder.

'Hell, I wish we could get off this thing right now.'

'You can, Val, just go ask the skipper.'

'Oh yeah sure, I thought people like that, you know like captains, were supposed to be officers and gentlemen—he's scary.'

'A gentleman is someone who gets out of the shower to take a leak.'

'You sound like Jeff.'

'Jeff! What a trip he is and he's not the only oddball on this old boat.'

'Ship.' She corrected. 'Who for instance?'

'Well, Spencer, he's smart, but well?'

'He's more than smart,' She said, 'genius for sure.'

'Yeah, but I think he's trying to put too much into what happened, I mean, about that prayer.'

'He has a great memory and—'

'But the prayer doesn't mean a thing Val, not a thing,'

'You know in Greek folklore, Mnemosyne's the personification of memory, he has that gift, I wish I had just a chunk of Spencer's recall power,'

'You have other good things.' Tommy said holding her closer.

'Stop, we're talking now,'

'Okay.' He teased—moving to leave.

She pulled him back. 'Where do you think you're going, boy?'

'I have to go anyway.'

'Do you have to?'

'I want to check things on deck, you know see if everything is . . .'

'You mean to see if anyone else has fallen over the side.'

'No, Val, no of course not, no more accidents.

'Accidents?'

'Yes, look it's time for us to get out of here anyway, go on back, I'll see you later.'

'Don't leave yet.'

'Oh—?'

On watch, Beth walked to the railing and looked over the side. She stared at the water for a moment or two then turned around quickly feeling the presence of someone close by. She stifled a gasp.

'Oh, Tommy, you scared me half to death.'

Tommy went to the rail and stood beside her.

'Sneakers don't make much noise I guess, I should have called you as I came up on deck, sorry.'

'Oh that's okay, I guess it's me, I'm sort of jumpy, you know?'

'Yeah, well everyone's a little jumpy. You all right?'

'Sure, I'm okay. You're up early, what time is it?'

'Just after four,' he told her.

'It sure is dark, should be lighter by now, I've had this watch before,' she said looking around the black sky, 'yeah, it should be lighter by now.'

'Where's Jim? I thought he was on this watch with you?'

'He is,' just went below, he'll be back in a minute, and we do the rounds together.'

'Want me to stay till he comes back?'

'Of course not,' she laughed, 'I'm a big girl now you know.'

'Okay then, see you, Beth.'

'Yeah, see you.'

The sun was well up over the horizon as the captain, in his usual position, in front of the wheel house, watched them closely as they appeared in groups of two's and three's hurrying to the deck. Quigley looked at each of them as they came up through one or another of the hatches. They shook their heads in silent answer to his questioning stare.

'Report!' The captain barked.

'Not on board, captain.' Quigley told him.

'The search?'

'Two searches captain, not on the ship.'

He considered the information for a moment then walked quickly to the railing on the starboard side and contemplated the ocean in the direction of the lazy wake behind the stern. They watched him and waited for his order to turn the ship around. Quigley, anticipating that order, pivoted a little to face them.

'All hands,' he murmured, 'stand by to go about.'

The captain did not to hear him. He stood motionless at the railing and peered out over the ocean. They waited ready to move fast when the order to turn the ship around would be given. It seemed as though he was about to do so as he turned to face them.

'Two searches,' Captain Burke said vaguely, 'very well, resume duties.'

He walked away toward the wheelhouse. They looked from one another in disbelief. Tommy felt as though he had been kicked in the stomach. Besides Jim he was the last one to see Beth and blamed himself for not staying with her even though she had told him not to. He felt enormous guilt and no matter that Val tried to do everything she could to assuage his feelings he knew too well what he should have done. And now that the captain was not going to order a search. He didn't hold back.

'Aren't you going to turn around?' Tommy yelled at him. 'Captain, you have to turn the ship around!'

The crew were quiet for another moment then began to call— one after another they shouted their protests. Even the quite reticent among them were encouraged into speaking out by the more vociferous.

'Turn around!'

'Go look for her!'

Voices were rising.

'Turn the fucken ship around!' Jeff bellowed.

'Captain!' Tommy walked right up and faced him. 'You have to turn back!'

Quigley tried to quiet them. 'Attention on deck!' He yelled but this time it didn't have any effect. All of one mind—they wanted the ship to go about—a search taken up immediately.

The captain turned to face them. His balanced gaze went from one to another until almost all of them had received a full measure of his icy stare.

'I don't have to do anything.' He said in a voice that was not his usual blunt form of speaking, milder and somewhat detached. His eyes became fixed on Tommy.

The unfamiliar voice startled him but Tommy went on.

'Captain, we need to turn back,' he said, 'and now!'

'That's right!' Jenny shouted, 'then we want to go back to Cape Upstart!'

The others took up the cry leaving no doubt their feelings be known.

'We want to go back to find Beth!'

'And then go home!'

The captain took a step toward them.

'Silence!' He yelled, his eyes glaring. 'Silence! All of you!'

Gone was the mild and detached voice, now it became loud, almost booming. The sound of his voice and his fierce countenance had a chilling effect. 'Silence!'

They fell quiet. Neither the captain nor anyone else said anything. The minutes passed. Then he moved closer to them and his speech changed dramatically again. It was neither mild nor thunderous. The harshness of before and soft words that preceded it disappeared to be replaced by something entirely different, a more reasonable, conciliatory tone.

'The sea,' he said, 'is a hard master, and we must yield to whatever the harvest of our labors is to be.' He seemed to drift and turned away from them to face the sea once more. The last words were spoken so softly that they could barely hear. 'That is all, the ship's company is dismissed.'

Val had not been one of the people shouting instead she had been observing the captain carefully. Captain Burke walked toward the aft hatchway leaving behind him the silence that he had demanded.

Eleven

'One at a time!'

It seemed as though everyone was talking at once and nobody was listening. Only a few of them sat on seats at the table Jeff and two others squatted on the floor and the rest of them stood or moved anxiously around the big cabin. It was supposed to be a meeting and some might have called it that, if it was, it was certainly a rowdy one. And it was beginning to get ugly. Some were shouting through the anguish at the loss of another friend merged with frustration and fear. Tommy, and Val were trying to get some kind of order out of the donnybrook that was going on, Jeff was not the only one that was loud. Spencer however, sitting at one end of the table, was thoughtful and said nothing. Many of them were a mess, bordering on hysteria.

Tommy was trying his best to quiet them. 'Come on,' he appealed, 'we'll never do anything this way, we have to stay as cool as we can.'

'Yes, all of us.' Val cut in.

'Why should you two clowns have all the say?' Jeff shouted above the racket.

'Everyone can say whatever they want,' Val countered, 'but let's try to do it one at a time, okay?'

'Quiet, quiet!' Tommy tried again this time with some success, they did settle down a bit.

'What are we going to do about Beth?' Debbie called from the end of the cabin near the galley.

That caused the uproar to restart.

'Yeah, what about Beth,' Wally said, 'she's the second, don't forget Alex!'

'I haven't forgotten Alex,' Tommy said, 'none of us have.'

Laura declared, 'We have to do something, don't we?'

'Damn right!' Someone yelled from the other end of the cabin.

'They must have been thrown off.' Jenny supposed, 'Quigley could have done it, he is crazy you know.'

'Maybe, or else they could have just fallen off,' Mary said weakly, 'I suppose it can happen.'

'People just don't fall off a ship one after another,' Matthew said, 'it makes no sense.'

'Maybe it was the captain,' Frank said speaking a lot more quietly than the others, 'did you see how he acted today? Erratic to say the least.'

'Yeah, maybe.' Debbie said.

'No, it has to be Quigley.'

'Think about it,' Tommy said shaking his head, 'Alex was a strong guy and Beth was no slouch either, they could have fought him off.'

'Stop saying she was!' Laura screamed then burst into loud sobs.

A few of them turned to look at her. There was a brief moment when everyone was quiet.

'Maybe it was both,' Jeff said, 'Crazy Quigley and the captain.'

'I have to agree with Jeff on that one,' Jenny nodded, 'could be both of them.'

'How about Sulkar? He would have no problem,' Frank asserted, 'he's bigger and stronger than any three of us, how about him?'

'He sure is big and strong.'

'That's true.'

'Well, whoever did it, we just can't go on, can we?' Wally said, 'like, we have to do something.'

'Right.'

'But why?' Karen said. 'Why is it happening?'

'Exactly.' Val spoke up, 'If we knew the why—'

'Yeah,' Wally thought, 'then we could stop the next . . .' He stopped abruptly but after a few seconds went on, 'Ah, I mean, if it is them we can't just let them pick us off one at a time.'

Some thought what Wally said made sense but the remark prompted another general outburst. A few opinions were thrown up then drowned out. Most of the ideas of what to do were for the most part too flawed to be considered seriously. And nobody was really listening. Then one voice shouted above the rest.

'Let's take over!'

A thought that might have been on some minds but Jeff was the one to say it. Everyone turned to stare at him. For a moment nobody spoke then suddenly every one had something to say. There was some enthusiasm for that idea around the cabin but again they began to make too much noise for anything else to be heard.

'Wait! Quiet down!' Tommy shouted, 'listen to me! Tell me this, if we did that who in the hell would run the ship?'

'We'll elect a captain.' Jeff yelled back at him.

'Who, you?' Tony and Kim said almost in unison.

'Sure, why not?' Jeff declared boldly.

'I suppose,' Jack said above the din, 'it's happened before, well hasn't it? You know, people falling overboard?'

'Sure, it's possible, I suppose . . .' Jenny backed him up, not strongly probably because she really didn't believe it. 'it's possible.' Her voice trailed away.

And so it went on. For almost two hours. Round and round, the same ideas were reiterated then rejected or debunked only to be reintroduced. They were getting nowhere. They could not find answers and had, by that time ran out of reasonable questions—were afraid—frustrated and home sick. Mostly afraid. And they didn't know what to do about it.

Spencer had been pretty much silent throughout the meeting, Tommy turned to him.

'Spencer, you haven't said anything?'

Spencer didn't reply right away, instead he looked around the cabin considering whether or not to say what he was thinking. Then he came to a decision.

'I don't know the answer as to what we should do either. But as to what has happened already I might say . . .'

'Yeah?'

'Okay, there is something, something that I didn't want to mention before.'

'Go ahead,'

'Well, I know this is going to sound off the wall to you—'

Jeff cut him off. 'Everything you say is off the wall.'

'Quiet Jeff,' Tommy said, 'let him talk, you've had your shot.'

'Who the hell made you king around here anyway?'

Jeff began a quick move from the other side of the cabin his hot temper erupting suddenly. Others stopped him from taking it any further.

'Sit down, Jeff,'

'Yeah, sit down and shut up,'

'Yeah, Jeff, shut the hell up!'

'Go ahead, Spencer,' Tommy prompted.

'You know as ship's clerk I check all the food, well, the first couple of days out I asked Quigley about the captain, I said he never draws anything from the pantry and Quigley said, well actually he giggled a bit, then he said, quote, oh that's all right, he said, the captain sees to his own rations. Then he giggled again in that way he does and walked away.' Spencer sat back in his chair and waited.

'You're not saying, not suggesting that—' Tommy began but Spencer cut him off.

'Offering, only offering a possibility.'

'No, Spencer, you're suggesting, that they are killing us one at a time, and, and, oh, please.'

'A possibility, that's all,'

'Now I know you're nuts,' Jeff put in.

'That is really weird, Spencer.' Tony said.

'Grotesque.' Jenny uttered and her whole body shook at the very thought of such a thing.

'What are they talking about?' Mary asked Wally.

'You don't want to know.'

'Yes, I do.'

Wally turned away from her. 'That's kind of cracked,' he said turning back to Spencer, 'isn't that seriously cracked?'

'Not at all,' Spencer said matter-of-factly, 'in fact it was quite common in the old days.'

'Yeah, the old days, and they were natives, cannibals.' Jeff said.

'Yes, that's true,' Spencer went on quietly, there was less noise in the cabin now, 'but cannibalism is not confined to any race.'

'Cannibalism!' Mary shrieked and then threw a hand over her mouth.

'Many times,' Spencer went on, 'shipwrecked sailors drew lots to see who would provide for the others survival, it was a common practice, and remember the plane crash in the Andes, you know that soccer team.'

'But those men were trapped on a mountain,' Wally said, 'and the one's that were well, you know, dead.'

'Are you saying the captain or Quigley? . . ' Tommy said.

'Or both, and maybe Sulkar too.' Spencer said quietly.

'That they have been killing and, no I can't buy that, no way,' Tommy said, 'end of discussion on that subject.'

'In fact,' Spencer continued anyway, 'I was talking to Frankie, during the first days on the ship, about Australian history, he and Jack told me stories about the old days in Australia, one instance, Frankie?'

'Well, yeah mate,' Frankie said, 'but I don't think, not these days, you know?'

'Why don't you tell them about it, it's very interesting?'

'Not to me, mate,' Frankie was reluctant.

'Why not,' Spencer prompted, 'most Australians probably know what happened anyway, its part of the early history of the country.'

'I don't,' Wally claimed, 'never heard of anything like that,'

'Well,' Frankie told him, 'yeah, it is history.'

'Okay,' Spencer cut in, 'there's also a book I read a while ago. . .'

'A book,' Jeff moaned.

'Well, okay,' Frankie said, 'there was this convict ah, Thomas Jones, in the early penal colony days of Australia, he escaped several times into the bush, always taking some other prisoners with him, but each time he was caught, he was alone. Once he said, at the time of his recapture, I'd have made it if I'd taken more rations with me.'

'Ahhh,' Mary whimpered.

'Don't think about it Mary,' Laura said, 'he's just trying to scare us.'

'Well on me, it's working.' Tony said.

Almost every one else at the table and around the cabin debunked the idea as too grotesque to be considered. Then, for the first time since the meeting had began, they were silent. An indicator perhaps to their vulnerability. Spencer thought he had a little more to add to what he had already said. *Might as well get it all out.*

'You're all forgetting something.' He said.

'Yeah, what?' Tony said. No one else seemed to want him to go on.

'The smell.'

After moments of absolute silence it was Debbie who asked Frank.

'What happened to him, the convict?'

'Oh, he was hanged, eventually.'

No doubt about it, it was a tumultuous two hours. However, one or two things were decided at the meeting. Feeling helpless to do otherwise, the crew would go about their duties as before. They would show up for watches and other work as though everything was normal, and one other important decision was reached.

On deck the next day Tommy came up to Jim as he had done with everyone on deck and not on duty below.

'Jim, who are you with?'

'Debbie, there she is by the forward hatch.'

'Okay, but you have to stay closer together.'

Jim closed the gap between them. 'Yeah, okay.'

'Good,' Tommy went on, 'you know the new rules, nobody, but nobody is to be on their own from now on. Hey Jeff! What the hell are you doing?'

'Nothin'.'

'You know what we decided. Everyone is on the buddy system. Someone has to watch out for you.'

'Someone is.' Jeff pointed upwards.

Wally was about a third of the way up in the rigging. He waved to Tommy.

'That's no good, Wally come on down from there!' Tommy turned to see that Quigley was eyeing them suspiciously. Wally came down to the deck lickety-split. He slid rather than climbed down out of the rigging by using the inside of his heels and his hands held loosely on the outside of the rope ladder. He slid to the deck faster than a fireman down the pole. Quigley had told him how to do it and had even demonstrated the old sailors trick.

'See, I can get to him in a second,' he said.

'Yeah but,' Tommy shook his head, 'can he get up there to you?'

'Oh yeah,' Wally said, 'you're right, I never thought it might be me.'

'It's new to all of us, just stay close.'

'Right, Tommy.'

'And we're going to change buddies all the time so that what we're doing won't be so noticeable to them, I mean to Quigley and Sulkar.'

'And the captain,' Wally told him, 'in an hour I switch, and then I'm with Laura.'

'And then I'm with, ah,' Jeff said, 'Tony, I'm with Tony.'

'Good. If we keep to this everything will be okay.'

That night in the main cabin.

'It's back Tommy.'

'Hold it down, Debbie.' He looked up from his food to see if any of the others had heard what she said.

'Can't you smell it?'

'Sure I can, but—'

'Pheewwuu! That stink again,' Jeff was the one to say it out loud and others were beginning to notice.

'Yeah, it stinks and it's—' Wally sniffed.

'Nauseating, yuck!' Debbie finished the sentence for him.

'Yeah, that too.'

'Smells kind of like, like burnt pork,' Jim suggested.'

'Pork, yeah it does smell like pork,'

'It's not as strong as last time though.' Wally thought.

Glorianna leaned closer to Wally in a way that he was the only one that would hear. 'Beth was smaller.'

Some others that had heard what she said turned to look at her, horrified but Glorianna was already on her way out of the cabin disappearing to wherever she disappeared to when not on watch with others.

Later, Tommy walked into the little alcove office that adjoined the main cabin where he found Spencer talking softly—there was no one else there.

'Talking to yourself Spencer? Not a good sign, buddy.'

'It's a popular misconception that talking to ones self leads to insanity, it does not. On the contrary, a great many scholars maintain that hearing the words out loud stimulates clarity.'

'Really?'

'Really, as in a lecture you are getting something clearly defined in the spoken word so in a way talking to yourself is lecturing to yourself, wouldn't you agree?'

'Sounds reasonable. You know Spencer, that was a really cold-blooded remark Glorianna made out there,'

'It was, but we have to face facts—it may be true.'

'I think we have to be careful around the others, you know if any of them hear something like again that, they could lose it.'

'You're probably right.'

'Tell me something, aren't you a little scared?' Tommy asked him.

'Sure, I'm scared like everybody else. You can't just stop people being scared. Anyway, we're all in the same boat.'

'Is that a joke?'

'Not in the least.'

Tommy punched him lightly on the arm good-naturedly. 'Because funny—it ain't.'

'You know, Tommy, I've had another thought, I wouldn't be surprised if—'

'All right let's hear it—just don't tell any of the others about your theories, okay? They're scared shitless now, I think some of them are about to lose it, you know, go completely crazy.'

'Ah yes,' Spencer scratched his temple with one finger for a second as if searching his memory, 'ah, yes,' he said after a few seconds, *"Quos deus vult perdere prius dementat"'*

'Meaning? My Latin is lousy.'

'A lawyer with lousy Latin? I thought Latin was part of the skill-kit for the job, sorry, profession?'

'It is, well, maybe not lousy, I have to brush up though—something about madness, right?'

'Yes. . . *Quos deus vult perdere prius dementat—those whom a god wishes to destroy, he first drives mad.'*

'Drives mad, huh?'

'Yes, drives mad. Anyway, as I was saying—'

Tommy a put a finger to his lips shushing Spencer down a bit so others who might be within earshot wouldn't hear.

'As I was saying, it would not surprise me,' Spencer said more quietly in response to Tommy's caution, 'I wouldn't be surprised if it's being done alphabetically, you know, A for Alex, B for Beth, see? Alphabetically, if so that would make Wally the last and—'

'Alphabetically?' Tommy thought about that.

'Yes, murder has been done that way before you know, and—' Spencer went on chattily with the cool, sang-froid of a completely disinterested observer rather than a potential murder victim, 'and,' he leaned in closer and whispered, 'Debbie would be the next.'

Twelve

Those not on watch were asleep, everyone—except Debbie. She lay awake with her eyes wide open, the reason for this sleeplessness was that a rumbling in her stomach had kicked in on her some time before—Debbie needed a snack. Slowly, she pulled the curtain back and got out of the bunk. Quietly, so as not to disturb anyone, almost everyone had trouble getting to sleep that night, she made her way aft and on through the gloomy half light of the main cabin and headed for the galley where there was no light at all.

Inside the galley, Debbie quickly poked around until she found what she was looking for—the big container that was stuffed with ship's biscuits. She began spreading a great glob of jelly over one of them. So intent on the jelly and biscuit preparation was Debbie that she was paying little attention to her surroundings. But something made her stop what she was doing. A sound? A movement? Something. She looked to the far end of the galley, trying to pierce the darkness. Was someone watching her through the blackness all the way from the aft galley door? She could feel a presence but could see nothing. Leaning her body toward the other door, she projected her voice in a raspy whisper.

'Who's there?' She listened for a moment. 'Is anyone there?'

It was said so softly that she could scarcely hear herself speak but the sound her own voice frightened her a little. Debbie resumed spreading the jelly, she couldn't be sure if she heard something or not but decided not to hurry and started to spread the jelly over a second biscuit deliberately. If she hurried that would be a sign to herself that she was about to panic and she was not going to let that happen. Bit by bit, methodically, she finished placing the sticky substance edge to edge over the biscuits. She put the container back in its place. Debbie stopped dead.

Standing absolutely still . . . listening. This time she was sure there was someone or something at the other end of the galley. The feeling was too strong to ignore. She put the knife down and began to back out of the galley. There was a movement. Even if she could not see anything or really even hear anything she could feel it for certain. Her first instinct was to run. But she didn't run, she couldn't. Her careful, backward walk did not become even a little faster. In fact, she moved slower and slower. And not once did her eyes leave the blackness at the other end of the galley. Holding the jelly covered biscuits in front of her—a totally useless weapon. *'Why,' she wondered, 'didn't she take the knife with her?'* Apple jelly biscuits would be no match for whoever, whatever, was about to strike.

She was almost out of the door and about to back into the main cabin. Feeling her way, Debbie began a slow turn but still kept her eyes glued to the dark at aft end of the galley. She knew the safety of the main cabin, although still gloomy, would, she was sure, put her at ease. Relieved to be almost out, she let the breath go that she had been holding for what seemed like minutes. Everything was okay, she had been silly to let her imagination run away with her like that. Debbie was turning completely around to face the cabin and began to move faster when she vaguely felt what she thought was a hand reaching out to her. Debbie screamed . . . a loud, penetrating shriek. Her hands flew to the sides of her face as she ran quickly into the main cabin only to run into someone approaching from out of the darkness. A light came on suddenly in the big cabin.

'Shit! Mathew you scared the daylights out of me!'

Coming in from the forward end of the cabin Wally turned up one of the lamps even higher. 'What's going on?' He said.

'I thought I heard someone and came in to check,' Mathew said, 'I'm sorry, Debbie, you okay?'

'Yeah, I think so, just let me catch my breath, and. . . '

In the lamplight she could see the biscuits laying jelly side down on the galley floor. 'Oh shit!' she wailed, 'my freaking biscuits!'

The crew, in two's and three's, no one was ever going to be alone any more, were on deck going about their duties. Light duties today, there were no explicit orders from Quigley or the captain. No fast speed runs, no more of the challenging re-rigging day and night. The pace was orderly and unhurried. The ship under light sail, the sea tediously placid, the weather, drearily calm. Quigley told them what to do and when to do it, nothing more. They had asked him time and again where they were heading, when would they reach land, but he had not responded or had simply walked away. Perhaps, many of them suspected, he didn't know any more than they did. At times the ship had a heading of due north but then the bow would be turned to the west and again, after some wind change or whatever, they weren't told what, the ship would veer to a more easterly direction. It could have been that the ship's direction was governed by the direction of the wind, they didn't know and there was no one who would tell them. It was all very confusing and perhaps what might have been under other circumstances, a period for them to be able to calm down—it had the opposite effect. The thought of not really knowing where they were and where they were going became increasingly unsettling. They saw no land and passed no ships.

Tommy, Spencer, Val and Jeff were still taking the captain's navigation class. They had tried to determine just where they were by quickly peeking at the charts that were sometimes laid out on the chart table at the aft section of the wheel house. But nothing conclusive came of it because the charts were too general and besides they were unmarked and that alone made them meaningless. Tommy however, noticed that every time they had come to the wheel house the captain was careful to put two of the charts that he had been working on into a cabinet in the wheelhouse. He would sometimes lock the cabinet and at other times, for some reason, he would not. Tommy felt sure that those charts would give them their position. Moreover, they had been unable to formulate any real plan therefore, no action was taken. It was almost tacitly agreed that they would more or less bide their time until some opportunity presented itself, just what kind of opportunity, they had no idea. Till then they would take every precaution they could think of to keep from losing another crew member, another friend. Each of them was determined that they would from now on look out for each other, would do more than simply watch each others back. And in doing so they did not want it to appear obvious. They talked endlessly among themselves of what had happened and of how could it be that they had the misfortune to be placed in such a horrible situation. Talk and more talk in twos and threes and factions developed so nothing was ever decided as a group.

Tommy, Val and Spencer kept whatever they thought they knew to themselves because they were afraid if they were to openly discuss some of it there may be outright panic and who knew what that might bring about. Particularly the theories that Spencer had come up with. The experience in the mess when he had recklessly announced that he thought cannibalism might be the answer to the missing Alex and Beth and the alarm that had caused made Tommy and Val more cautious, especially Tommy. Val did tell him that she thought it might be better to have things out in the open all round. But in the end, she went along with him and mentioned none of it to the others.

'Oh, Tommy, how I need to get off this boat.'

'Along with me and everyone else,' he said quietly while checking others working on the deck or hanging around nearby. 'To tell the truth, I think most of them are about ready to crack. Spencer thinks we're all for it.'

'He could be right,' Val frowned, 'two people, gone, and I know I must have said this a thousand times, if they are not accidents, who's doing it?'

'One of them or . . . I don't know . . . Quigley?'

'Quigley, well, sometimes he's okay I mean not erratic, especially when it comes to sailing and things like that, other times, it's like he's off his rocker.'

'Yeah,' Tommy said, 'but you should be able to see if he's insane right? I mean, as a Psychologist?'

'It takes more than casual observation. Anyway, there are all kinds of insanity. Clearly Quigley isn't stable but is he insane? I don't think he's all that disturbed. But it's not an act either.'

Tommy rubbed his eyes, took in a deep breath and then shook his head. 'Hell, I don't know,' he said, 'he's nuts— he's not nuts, at any time you can take your pick.'

'It's not always a clear choice, Tommy.'

'But when you think about it, wouldn't it take someone crazy to do it, I mean Alex and Beth, throwing them over the side, and wouldn't he have to be crazy?'

'He or they.' Val said.

'Or they, yes, one or both crazy.'

'Quigley's not a mental incompetent, Tommy, I'm sure of that. Oh yeah, he's a little off sure, maybe a lot off, but not completely senseless. Many people are a little, let us say, quirky, they tend to behave in a quirky manner but that doesn't necessarily mean that they are deranged to any extent. Like Quigley, he's quirky all the time which might mean he's just quirky.'

'Sometimes a cigar is just a cigar, right?'

'Ah, quoting an alleged Freud remark, huh? Have you been boning up in my territory, mister?'

'I'll stick to lawyerin', thanks. So it doesn't mean he's crazy?'

'Crazy is an all-purpose term, vernacular really,' Val clarified, 'besides, there are a great many types of mental illness with capricious levels of effects ranging from the simply those who are slightly off all the way through to the certifiable right on up to the uncontrollably insane.'

'So it doesn't mean because someone acts crazy that he's actually crazy?'

'No,' Val answered, 'there is one recognizable peculiarity and that is when a person changes character completely at times. That can be one of the many classifications of insanity.'

'Becomes a different person?'

'Yes, there are cases like that.'

'And that would be schizophrenia?'

'Right, Tommy, schizophrenia.'

'Dangerous?'

'Very dangerous.'

'Then it has to be one of them, Val, can you—?'

'You want me to keep an eye out for anything?'

'Yeah, why not?'

'Well, of course I have been doing that automatically. But there would have to be a clear sign of, well, something recognizable but Tommy, if I did notice something, what would, what could, we really do about it?'

'Hmmm—'

'Moving into your area of expertise, if, I say if,' Val went on, 'we could reach a port and turn them over to, to the cops, I suppose?'

'Yeah, I've thought about that but what could we tell them? What proof do we have that Alex and Beth were not lost overboard, that it was just accidents, nothing, no solid proof.'

'I guess so.'

'The best we can do is watch out for each other, that is all of us, until we can get off this friggin ship.'

'Isn't it strange,' Val said thoughtfully, 'we took this trip for us to have a chance to decide our future, now we're not sure if we'll even survive.'

Tommy reached out to her and she held his hand tightly.

'We'll survive.'

While they were talking, Jenny, further along the deck, was checking herself with a small compact mirror. Sleepless nights or at best, restless half sleep had caused dark circles to appear under her pretty eyes. Jenny stopped what she was doing and looked more deeply into the mirror. She began to stare at something else that had caught her attention. The compact slipped from her hand and fell to the deck with a clatter and began to roll away as she spread her fingers wide apart. A loud whimper issued from her. The whimper turned suddenly into a scream, long and loud, all the while staring at the fallen compact.

'What is it, Jenny?' Debbie said, jolted by the outburst as were the two others girls with her.

'What happened? Jenny, what is it?'

Val went up to her. Those that were on deck began to come forward and crowd around. Jenny backed away from them, her eyes wide in terror staring at the mirror now lying on the deck. They tried to restrain her and calm her down but she pushed them away until she had backed herself hard up against the railing. Such was her concentrated stare at the compact that Jenny didn't realize where she was. She was about to tip over backwards and into the sea. Val and the others became aware of the imminent danger as they moved toward her. Val could see that any sudden move would no doubt send her over the rail. Val put her arm up halting the others in their movement toward Jenny. Then, she alone went slowly toward the troubled girl who was about to go into the water. Her piercing scream had unnerved everyone and was affecting them more and more as it continued, it had to stop. When she was close enough to grab one of Jenny's arms. She looked blankly at Val for a moment then, the scream fragmented into a wretched sobbing. Some of the others led her away from the rail, to the hatchway and down into the main cabin.

Tommy picked up the compact and looked into the mirror. He could detect nothing that could have thrown Jenny into such a frenzy. Then he positioned himself to where Jenny had been sitting and looked backward through the mirror. Panning and pointing the compact aft to the rear mast then back again to the ship's bell. In the mirror he could see what had taken Jenny to near hysteria.

'What is it, Tommy?'

Tommy didn't answer instead he turned his head slightly to his right. He could see the captain watching him from the after deck. They looked at each other for a moment then the captain went on into the wheel house and closed the hatch behind him. Tommy handed the mirror to Val and turned her around so that she was facing toward the bow. Val saw it faster than he did.

'Oh, my God!'

Hanging from the front of the wheel house, the ships bell, engraved into the brass, the name of the ship, *Erehwon* reflected through the mirror—nowhere.

Tommy could hear Spencer call softly but couldn't see where the call was coming from. He looked around the main cabin but the only people in there were the mess hands on that duty and Mary, one of the cooks passing though on her way to the galley.

'In here, Tommy.'

'That you Spencer? Where the hell are you?'

'Come in here.' Spencer pulled the heavy curtain aside and at the same time scanned the cabin to make sure that they were not being observed. Then he pulled Tommy into the alcove, the small area forward of the main cabin that served as the library. Spencer checked once more to see that no one was watching then snapped the curtain shut.

'What?'

'Listen, Tommy,' he said quietly as he checked again that the curtain had completely shut them off from the main cabin, 'Glorianna wants to tell us something.'

Tommy saw now that Glorianna was standing just inside the alcove half hidden at the very end of the area.

'I'm not sure I can take another *something*.' Tommy said in a loud voice.

'Hold it down, shush!'

Val drew the curtain back and entered. 'What's up?'

'For Christ's sakes, Spencer, it's only Val.'

'Gee thanks, that's me, only Val.'

'Spencer has something.'

'Not me, Glorianna.' Spencer said, 'She has something to tell us.'

'Is it how to get off a ship?'

'That would be okay with me.' Val agreed.

'What she has to say, is I think, interesting,' Spencer turned to her. 'Okay Glorianna, tell them.'

Glorianna dressed in the usual black caftan and looking as furtive as ever flashed her dark eyes as she spoke.

'What has happened is the work of a Triton.'

'A who?'

'A what?'

'A Triton . . . let me explain.' Glorianna said taking her time and speaking softly. 'Triton, sometimes said to be descended from Poseidon and Amphitrite, is a marine deity of the lower order . . .'

Tommy opened both his hands palms up and looked at her. 'For Christ's sakes Glorianna, mythology!'

'Tommy, let her speak, go ahead, Glorianna.' Val seemed more inclined to listen while Tommy at first shook his head and then shrugged for her to go on.

'Triton is a marine deity of the lower order and the herald of Neptune in which capacity he is uses a long, twisted shell—' Glorianna paused for a second to emphasize the point and then

. went on, 'A twisted shell that he uses to blow a gentle note when the seas are to be hushed to rest.' Glorianna paused again for a minute to make sure that she had their attention, she had Val's to some extent but Tommy seemed like he was about ready to leave.

'Glorianna, I don't see . . .'

Ignoring Tommy's interruption, Glorianna went on.

'Remember those sounds we heard just before Alex and Beth disappeared? And the sea became so calm?'

Tommy didn't want to encourage her and was about to interrupt her again but noticed that Val seemed like she was being lured in as Glorianna spoke in throaty tones her voice rising and falling but still within the confines of a raspy undertone.

'A gentle note—a gentle note to calm the sea!' She stopped cold and looked at them carefully for a moment again then went on. 'Listen to me—Triton is a monster who by his wantonness and voracity renders the sea and those who sail on it—dangerous.'

Glorianna indicated by her body language that she was waiting for them to say something but several moments passed before anyone said anything. Val broke the silence.

'What do you think, Tommy?' Val placed a hand on his arm.

'Wait a sec, Val . . . Glorianna, we have to be realistic about all that's been occurring and what we think might be going on. For all we know, both of them were accidents, maybe they did fall off the ship, we just don't know what happened do we?'

'You are wrong! I know what happened to them—' Glorianna cried domineeringly and her eyes widening. Her sudden outburst forced them into stillness for a moment. Then Glorianna went on more calmly. 'Tritons are of human form down to the hips, the lower part of them, is the tail of a dolphin but—but only when in the sea.' She had stopped again looking carefully at each of them one at a time. A moment passed while they contemplated what Glorianna had said.

'Mythology.' Tommy finally muttered.

Glorianna ignored him and had more to say. 'When in danger, Triton will blow a loud blast from the shell and the sea will become agitated into ferocity. The Triton becomes the personification of the roaring sea.' She leaned back and away from them—her eyes narrowed to slits — as she repeated this time in a whisper, 'by his wantonness and voracity renders the sea and those who sail on it—dangerous.'

Val and Tommy were a little stunned. Georgiana's discourse had been, to say the least, compelling.

'But it is still mythology, Tommy said,' or legend.'

'Triton is real, but yes,' Glorianna conceded, 'there is some legend, Triton appeared in a Boeotian legend, Triton attacked the local women while they were bathing in the lake. But in answer to their prayers Dionysus came to them and drove off Triton. Triton also plundered the shores of the lake, until the day when a jug of wine appeared on the shore. Drawn by the smell of the wine, Triton went up to it and drank. He fell asleep there and then . . . Triton was killed with an axe.'

Spencer looked for their reaction.

Tommy sat down on the floor, drew his knees up, placed elbows on them and cupped his chin in his hands.

'Interesting legend but nothing to do with what's been going on.' He said finally. 'Oh, I'll admit there are some coincidences, the sound we heard, the calm sea, yeah, but that proves nothing, Glorianna, just a few things that are coincidental. How do you know about all this anyway?'

'I know.' Glorianna told him.

'How?'

'I just know.'

'But Glorianna —'

'And something else,' she cut him off, 'Triton does not create offspring in the way humans do.'

Tommy and Val looked at each other for a moment.

'What do you say Tommy?' Spencer said, 'it's kind of . . .'

'It's mythology! Don't get carried away Spencer, for Christ's sake, it only a bunch of legend and myth. Okay, so we heard the sound of something, a flute in my book, or even a voice, yeah, it could have been a voice . . . and yeah, the sea did get calm I'll grant you that, which I think was a coincidence, but answer me this then, when the sea was rough, right? Did we ever hear sound from any horn. Did we?' He looked at her, 'Glorianna, its myth and nothing to do with what's been going on with us, trust me.'

'Well,' Spencer cut in, 'here at least we have some evidence to help us figure out what's been happening and give us maybe an inkling of what might happen, you have to concede that don't you?'

'No I don't! That's not evidence, Spencer, it's at best speculation and we don't know enough to speculate on any of it, no way.'

'Oh, I agree with you it is weird.' Spencer would not be put off easily, 'But everything about this ship is weird isn't it? And think about this, when you can eliminate everything that's realistic and logical, what are you left with? . . . The unreal, the illogical.'

Tommy shook his head and got to his feet.

'I can't buy that, there has to be an answer that makes sense.'

'Hmmm,' Spencer murmured, 'Triton can't make offspring and was killed with an axe, interesting. What do you think, Val?'

'Where do I stand?' Val, seemingly undecided, 'What Glorianna says is interesting and I'm sure she believes in it entirely.

But I want Tommy to be right, no, that's not correct, I need, I really need Tommy to be right. I'm sure Glorianna knows what she's talking about—'

'Forget it Val,' Tommy scoffed, 'with all due respect Glorianna, it's a crock.'

Glorianna looked from one to the other of them. A tight little movement of her mouth that was accompanied by a scornful murmur appeared on her white face. Then she turned quickly and disappeared through the curtained entrance.

Tommy waited until he was sure Glorianna was out of hearing distance before turning to Val.

'You don't believe any of that do you?'

'I believe, that Glorianna believes it. And you can't disparage someone else's beliefs, whatever you may think — you can't just shoot them down.'

'Why the hell not?'

'Tommy, yes, I deal with reality—but a fantasy, even a delusion, in someone's mind is of a certain reality, it has a measure of veracity, off actuality, and I have to respect that.'

'You're quite right,' Spencer agreed, 'you can't just dump on something that someone else believes in that you don't have knowledge of.'

Tommy wouldn't go along with any of it. 'Again, why not?'

'Epistemology, as I'm sure you know,' Spencer went on, 'is one of the three main branches of modern western philosophy, others being ethics and metaphysics. Epistemology is the philosophical discipline that considers the nature, basis, and limits of knowledge. And ancient Greek philosophers examined the relations between knowledge, truth and belief and the question of whether knowledge exists independently of the knower.'

'What you're saying,' Tommy said, 'is that there are things that exist that we don't know about?'

'Oh, there are, there has to be things that we just don't know about,' Spencer said emphatically, 'our knowledge is definitely limited. And epistemology is asking us to consider what are, at times, three unconnected things . . . knowledge . . . truth . . . and . . . belief.'

They stood silently for a few moments.

'Who knows.' Tommy sighed.

Spencer nodded. 'Exactly.'

Tommy shook his head and smiled. 'I'm going to miss these little chats, Spencer.'

'Is that remark meant to be a tad facetious?'

'No, it's meant to be entirely and unequivocally facetious, and I hope, Spencer, you don't have any more surprises for us.' Turning to Val. 'Next he'll be telling us the ships haunted, that it's a phantom ship.'

'Hmmm,' Spencer rubbed his chin, 'a phantom ship, specters, spirits, the supernatural,' Spencer's eyebrows lifted and his voice lowered, 'ghosts!'

Thirteen

It was three hours into the eight to midnight watch, Jim was at the helm. Tommy Spencer and Val were in the wheelhouse with him, outside and nearby, Wally and Laura. Quigley could be seen at the forward end of the middle deck. He was standing quite still staring back toward the stern of the ship. But at irregular intervals he would make his way back from the upper fore deck then back aft, usually not quite as far as the wheel house. There he would stop for a few minutes then do it all again.

'Tommy,' Val whispered, fully aware of Quigley's sharp hearing, 'this doubling and tripling up on the watches is getting to be too hard on everyone.'

'I know it is, but it is the only way we can be safe, we have to do it.'

'Safe, sure,' Wally said through the open wheelhouse side window, 'but how long can we take it?'

'Keep it down,' Laura warned, 'Quigley's not that far away.'

Quigley was on his way back to the aft of the ship but he stopped and turned toward the bow again. He had done this several times, sometimes he seemed to hurry along the deck, at other times he would walk more leisurely, it was impossible to predict, fast, slow stand still or move around—there was no pattern to his actions and it was making them nervous. He was just standing there now and had been for a few minutes. Suddenly with a jerky movement, he resumed the walk. Of course it was the normal watch keeping duty but they wondered if there was a reason for some changes tonight. He didn't go as far as the top of the fore deck, he usually did, so that meant that he always had a good view of the wheelhouse and presumably, those inside. And at times, when he was close enough, he would probably be able to hear them talking. His beady little eyes and sharp hearing missed nothing. They had to be careful. And some of them, thought that he looked a little more on the crazy side tonight, his eyes squinting and staring out of an otherwise blank face. But Tommy said that was probably their imagination working overtime. To him he looked the same as always.

'How much longer can we keep doubling up on the watches?' Wally murmured.

'For as long as it takes to get to some port, island, anywhere—back to Australia.'

Tommy and the others lowered their exchanges to a whisper. The sea was exceptionally tranquil so any noise or talking could be heard clearly at almost any distance. The only sounds were from a sporadic light zephyr that rattled gently through the shrouds and an occasional ships timber creak.

'How long?' Laura said so softly that she was almost to the point of merely mouthing the words, they were all whispering now, 'we can't keep this up.'

'Sooner or later he has to make for a port,' Tommy said, 'he has to.'

'Why don't we know where we are, anyway?'

'They don't tell us much, Laura, when we ask, he doesn't answer, he has Quigley tell us what the compass heading is that's all.'

'That's right,' Val said, 'and he's changing it all the time. It would be a help just to know where we are.'

'We, Spencer and me, have been trying to figure it out. We could be deep in the South Pacific, or a few miles off the horizon there,' Tommy pointed in a wide arc, 'could be the coast of Australia or an island, take your pick,'

'Or any place in between.' Spencer said.

'Or anywhere.' Wally murmured.

'That's about it.' Tommy agreed.

'Hell, I'm scared.' Laura moved even closer to Wally.

'Just stay together,' he told her, 'we'll be okay.'

Below the mess cabin was empty, dark and almost soundless the only noise of any kind was a soft, scraping coming from the galley. Again, Debbie was spreading jelly over one of the ship's hard biscuits. Debbie, her concentration directed on the knife and biscuit, was careful not to make any noise. As usual her attention was focused on the biscuit so didn't realize what was reaching to her until it was too late. One hand almost encircled her throat while the other clamped tightly over her mouth. Debbie's eyes widened in terror. The hands grabbed her so suddenly that she had no time to call out or run. The unyielding grip on her neck and mouth made it almost impossible for her to have any movement other than her legs. Almost at once the feeling came over her that she was about to die. And it occurred to her that she should give up and make it a quick end. But instead she began a struggle. If she was going to die she would not go quietly. She tried kicking out in all directions, behind her especially but to no avail. Debbie was a strong young woman but she realized at that instant that no matter what she did she was going to die anyway. She was being pulled back toward the aft galley door. By reflex, instinct or courage, or something else, she struggled. She and her attacker crashed into the rear galley door slamming it shut. The attacker would have to use one of his hands to try to open it while holding onto Debbie with the other. Debbie thought she might soon lose consciousness and there was nothing she could do about it. Now, she thought, this was it—time to let go—time to die.

'Wally,' Tommy whispered, 'I want you to let us know when Quigley is going up to the fore deck, okay? If he turns to come back you and Laura to go up to him, talk to him, got it?'

'What shall I say?'

'Anything, just keep him busy for as long as you can, even for a couple of minutes, okay?'

'He sure looks weirdo tonight. Okay, you're with me Laura?'

'Absolutely.'

Tommy needed a few minutes to get into the locker.

'You going for the chart?'

'If I can.'

'Okay, he's moving away, up the deck,' Wally called back softly.

'Go for it.' Spencer told Tommy.

Tommy knelt down on the deck and checked first to see if the chart cupboard was locked, it wasn't.

'So far so good, it's open,' he whispered, 'this is our lucky night.'

From somewhere deep inside her Debbie found a will to stay alive and was struggling to keep from being dragged backwards by holding on grimly to a bench railing. The attacker had not yet been able to reopen the door, with only the use of one hand

fumbling behind his back to find the latch and the other holding
and trying to drag backward the struggling girl.

'Okay Spencer, there are only two charts here, lets get them
out, lay them on the floor, you hold down that end, Val, what's
Quigley doing?'

'He's still going the other way . . . Wally?' Val called to him in
the loud whisper that they were all speaking in, 'Wally, be ready
to go keep him busy if he starts to come back, okay?'

'You bet, I got him in sight.'

Tommy and Spencer, down on their knees unrolled the first
chart and laid it out on the deck. Tommy began to trace a copy
over it. Spencer glanced up over the window cowling to see that
Quigley was not close enough to see them, in so doing his hand
moved enough to let the map curl up again.

'For Christ's sakes Spencer!'

'Oh, sorry, I got it, go ahead.'

Debbie knew that the plate rack was near her on the long
bench. It was an old fashioned affair made of heavy wood with
a bottom and three sides that held the plates in place. There
was room enough between the slats to allow the galley people
to reach into it and draw out the heavy dinner size crockery,
one at a time. It was free standing on the bench and secured
only by the two inch fiddles that surrounded all the tables and
benches keeping things like the rack in place in times of rough
weather. She thought if she were able to wrap her legs around
the rack there was a good chance of toppling it. But that would
mean if she made the attempt and missed her legs would no
longer give her the leverage she had now and that she would be
more easily dragged out of the galley. It was black as ink in the

galley but she knew approximately where the rack was. It was incredible that the sounds of the struggle she was putting up had not already roused someone but it had not. Debbie knew that she would have only one shot. If she tried and missed that was the end, she would be killed. It seemed as though the hands had been gripping her forever and at the same time the precious seconds she needed to save herself were passing so quickly. She made up her mind in one of those seconds that this would be her only chance.

'What was that? Did you hear something?'

Tommy wasn't sure if he had heard something or not. Val and Spencer listened for a moment. Spencer shook his head.

'No, keep going, do the second map, quickly.'

'I haven't finished this one yet.'

Debbie lifted both her legs at the same time. Luck, for the moment, was on her side, her legs wrapped around the plate rack. But the rack refused to move. She tightened her legs in a death grip but since she no longer had any leverage, her feet were completely off the floor—still the rack would not budge. Then the latch lifted and the door was opened wide. Ironically it was the fact that she was at that moment pulled backwards with a tremendous jerk that finally dislodged the rack. It began to move toward the edge of the bench.

'Tommy!' Val whispered suddenly, 'Quigley's on his way back! He just pushed past Wally and Laura without stopping!'

'Okay give me the other chart, I need a few more seconds!'

'Hurry!'

'He's coming back!' Spencer said, 'quickly! He's moving faster this time!'

The rack tumbled off the bench and smashed to the galley floor. The sound of the shattering plates could be heard throughout the ship—even by those on deck.

Quigley turned his head toward the sound and began to run. 'What was that?' He called on the run toward the wheelhouse his eyes wide and darting around crazily.

'What the hell?' Tommy said in a loud voice, there was no more whispering now.

'Below!' Wally shouted, and began to run toward the hatchway, 'it came from below!'

'Quick put them back,' Spencer told Tommy, 'Quigley's almost here.'

'Another few seconds.

'He's right here!'

'Okay!' Tommy yelled as he rolled the charts and stuffed them in their place and slammed the door shut with a thump, 'You three stay here, and don't separate! Val, Spencer, come on!'

'Right behind you — go!'

They rushed down the aft companionway into the main cabin. Others began streaming out of the sleeping quarters by the time Tommy and Val arrived at the galley entrance that led off the mess cabin.

Seconds before that Debbie had been dropped to the floor at the sound of the crashing plates, and the rear galley door slammed behind her attacker after he had fled through it. Tommy and the others ran in to find Debbie crawling toward them and pointing at the door. Val went to her. Tommy moved cautiously to the door then pulled it open with a jerk. In the companionway beyond the door, the giant Sulkar came toward him. They stared at each other for a moment—Sulkar stopped and stood quite still. Tommy slammed the door shut and rammed the bolt into the locked position. Without waiting another instant, he ran to the other door leading down to the forward end of the main cabin. He quickly banged that door shut and shoved the bolt home with a clatter of metal on metal.

'Jeff! You and Spence, go tell the others, everyone get into the main cabin. Get the others off the deck and out of the wheel house.' He called loudly, 'everyone come down here, now!'

'I'm on it!'

Jeff didn't waste any time and started to run with Spencer right behind. Tommy shouted over his shoulder, 'Get them all to come down the forward hatch and we'll let them in that way, somebody get something to jam against the other door, hurry!'

The galley door and both entrances to the main cabin had been locked and barricaded with a lot of the cabin furniture. Anything that was movable was stacked or jammed against the entrances. That meant though, that the only access to the sleeping cabins and toilets was through a small hatch that was also barricaded but they would open when it was necessary to go in there and secure the hatchway again immediately afterward. They had to have some rest after the previous forty eight hours of doubling and tripling of the watches not to mention the attack on Debbie which had a profoundly debilitating effect on almost everyone after the initial shock had worn off. Another reason they figured they needed to be rested as much as possible was that no one knew what lay ahead, what else might be in store for them.

Debbie, with several visible injuries, a severe bruising around the neck and her right shoulder, told them about the attack. Curiously, she was the one among them with the higher spirits. She had been though a shocking ordeal and was thankful that she had come through it all with so little injury. But as so often happens a person who has survived an ordeal would experience a sensation not only relief but a feeling close to euphoria. Debbie's spirits were so surprisingly high that without really being aware of it she was able to lift the spirits of others a little. The all-pervading fear that was so evident in the main cabin was only outdone by the desperate need of sleep. However no one wanted to go the bunks section of the lower deck. They preferred what they thought to be the security of the main cabin, and after a number of parleys that is what they decided to do. Safety in numbers and stay within a tight group. Even so, drained though they were, it was decided without complaint that some of them had to stay up to keep watch. One attack had been thwarted by Debbie's ingenuity and courage and perhaps some arrant luck. But every one of them knew that was not the end of it. There would be more of the same or things that could happen that they, at the moment, could not bring themselves to contemplate. Nevertheless they must take whatever safety measures they could if they were ever to get off the ship alive. Right now they needed to be safe, to rest and wait. Wait for what? They had no idea. Most could only think that the attempt of Debbie's life would not be the last of its kind.

First they had satisfied themselves as to the stability of the barricades then a few of them talked for a time about the incident.

Before that of course, they had listened with rapt attention while Debbie related the story in detail. There followed the usual debate on what they should do. But this time it was over with in short order and again, as usual, it was like all the other times they had tried to resolve the situation, nothing was accomplished. Moods and actions varied. Tommy, apprehensive but assuaging, neither agreeing nor disagreeing with anything—Val, anxious but solicitous, counseling those who were most distressed—Jeff, angry and vociferous but coming up with nothing—and Spencer, contemplative.

For whatever lay ahead, rest was essential, those who were to stand watch were divided into pairs. Two of them would take up guard duty at each door in two hour shifts while the others rested, hopefully sleep. They did the best they could under the circumstances—there were no complaints. It was a strange looking crew laying as they were in such a variety of positions throughout the cabin. Some were able to drift into a fitful slumber, for others, sleep came only minutes at a time then they would wake with a start, and try again. Jeff was among the very few who were able to get to sleep without too much trouble. Tommy shook his head 'Take a look, Val, sleeping like a baby.'

Tommy and Val were of course together. They had nominated themselves to take the first watch, their station, guarding the aft companionway door. Spencer sat upright on the floor near them also awake. They talked softly not because Quigley or Sulkar might hear, but what they were saying might easily cause alarm among the others.

'At least we know now that it is not Quigley if nothing else,' Val was saying her voice barely audible, 'he was on deck with us, right?'

'Yes, but,' Tommy countered, 'he could still be part of it.'

'He could very well be.' Spencer agreed.

'We do know,' Val said, 'that we have to consider all three of them as suspect.'

They were careful not to disturb those near them. Spencer who took up the conversation once more. 'Okay, there's a few things I want you to consider, you want to hear?'

'I think I know what you 're going to say.' Tommy told him. 'All right, but keep it down.'

'Of course,' he looked around before going on, 'Debbie told us that she didn't actually see who it was that attacked her right?'

'It was Sulkar,' Val said shaking her head, 'we all know it was, Tommy saw him.'

'Tommy saw him outside the galley, not inside, outside. Certainly, it was probably him but remember Debbie couldn't be certain, she said it was him yes, but she didn't for a fact see who it was, did she?'

'Yeah but who else?' Tommy said, 'he was right there outside the rear galley door, it must have been him. It was definitely Sulkar.'

'You're probably right, but we should consider all the possibilities shouldn't we?'

'What other possibilities are there? Sulkar, the captain and Quigley?'

'Go on, Spencer,' Val urged, 'I'm wide awake, and I know I won't be able to sleep, go ahead,'

'Putting aside for the moment that we are agreed that it was Sulkar,' Spencer looked at them both. 'We know the captain could probably be eliminated as a suspect at least for tonight's episode because of Debbie's account of what went on, and Quigley, as we know, was on deck where we could see him at all times, right?'

'That's right,' Val agreed, 'so if the captain is out and Quigley is out, Tommy saw Sulkar so it has to be him, Spencer, two out of three leaves, Sulkar.'

'Yes, but you know how big he is?' Spencer said shaking his head, 'I believe he could pick Debbie up in a second, he has to be the strongest man I've ever seen, how come he didn't get it over with instantly?' Spencer hadn't finished yet. 'Then let me ask you this, have you considered the possibility that there might be other people on this ship?'

Val and Tommy didn't answer right away instead they looked at each other.

'Gee, I never thought of that, did you Tommy?' Val said.

'Well, I guess there is some parts of the ship that we have never seen.'

'Could someone be hiding all this time where we couldn't see them,' Val supposed, 'Well, it's possible I guess, but,' she hastened to add, 'in my opinion, highly doubtful.'

'Only a possibility,' Spencer conceded, 'remember we are only exploring possibilities,'

'Okay Spencer,' Tommy propositioned, 'it's possible but at least tonight we have something tangible, not like Alex and Beth, we don't know for sure about them do we? But now this thing tonight is out in the open, not a mystery, we know someone, we think Sulkar, grabbed Debbie, and that's a fact.'

A sound, what was it? A spar jarred slightly with a sudden gust of wind? It was nothing that they hadn't heard hundreds of times over the last days and nights but in the confines of the cabin and the stillness of this awful night it sounded—different. Three pairs of eyes stared up as though they could see through the heavy beamed overhead to the deck and wondered what might be going on up there. The others, those not on guard, huddled in twos and threes, prepared to wait out the long night sleeping or if not, at least in silence.

'I've been trying to think of something else,' Tommy said, 'anything else that might be, you know, like a reason for all this.'

'Yes?' Val wanted to hear this.

'Yeah, I thought about that too.' Spencer said. 'But what you said before, about things being out in the open now, does there have to be a reason?'

'There has to be a reason for everything,' Val said adamantly, 'and that, Spencer, means everything.'

'Absolutely.' Tommy agreed. 'Things just don't happen for no reason at all, do they?'

Spencer thought for about a minute and shook his head.

'I'm sorry I can't categorically agree with you on that. There are things that do happen for no logical reason or for no obvious reason, but things do happen that have no explanation and Tommy, that's a fact.'

'Well, Val?' Tommy looked at her.

'True,' Val had to try to see Spencer's point, 'there are some things that happen that cannot be rationally explained.'

They fell quiet for several minutes. Spencer finally broke what had become utter silence in the cabin.

'Very well, lets review. Let's just say for now, the captain is out, Quigley is out, and just for a moment, please for a moment, let us say Sulkar is out, okay? For all we know Sulkar could have been on his way to help Debbie after hearing the ruckus . . . don't shake your head, you saw him outside the door, he could have been on his way to help, it's a possibility.'

Tommy shook his head again. But Spencer went on anyway.

'Okay, so Sulkar is out, the captain is out, Quigley was on deck with us, he is out. Then let us agree that there is no one else on board the ship, Okay?'

Tommy thought about it for a moment.

'Okay?' Val urged him to go on.

'Yes but—' Tommy interrupted.

Spencer held up a hand in a gesture that would allow him finish his thought.

'Let me ask you to think about this then. Since the first day when we got on board this vessel, this is the only time we have all, I mean everyone in this cabin, have been together at one time?'

'What exactly do you mean?'

'I mean, simply put, this is the only time that each and every one of us can be accounted for.'

'Are you saying someone in this cabin is responsible?'

'We have to consider all the possibilities.'

'No way,' Val said, 'I'd never buy that, would you Tommy?'

'Me neither, it's not anyone here in this cabin, I'm sure of that,' Tommy gazed around in the half light recognizing even those of his shipmates whose face he could not see, by their posture, clothing or something else. He knew these people. Then he added, 'at least, I think I'm sure.'

'Just considering all the possibilities.' Spencer said and then moved away a little, made himself as comfortable as he could and was asleep in minutes.

Tommy pulled Val closer. 'You thinking about what Spencer said?'

'No. I was thinking about when we started on this trip down to Australia. Remember, how eager we were?'

'Oh, yeah, we were.'

'Val sighed. 'That's one plane I wish we'd missed.'

Fourteen

'Ahoy! Ahoy down there!'

Val woke with a start.

'It's Quigley!' She shook Tommy awake, 'Tommy! It's Quigley!'

The others stirred and began to move from the positions that they had slept in. Fear and foreboding took a strong grip on them all over again. It was early morning and Quigley was shouting to them from the top of the companionway down to the locked and barricaded door.

'Ahoy below!'

Tommy went quickly to the bottom of the companionway to check first that the door was still secure. Frank and Wally were on that guard duty but sound asleep, now they stirred.

'What do you want?' Tommy shouted through the door.

'The captain wants you, on deck, all hands on deck, captain's orders.'

'No way!'

There was a pause before Quigley called again.

'He wants to talk to you.'

'Forget it!'

'Better do as you're told, boy.' Quigley answered. 'Captain's ordered all hands on deck.'

Tommy looked at the others who had gathered around. Jeff shook his head to indicate what he thought of the idea of going up to the deck. Others did the same.

'We'll talk it over.' Tommy shouted.

'Make up your mind boy and be quick about it, the captain ain't the most patient man in the world.'

Tommy motioned them and they moved back into the main cabin where the rest of them were waiting.

'Any ideas?' He said when they were clustered around.

'I think—' Spencer began but Jeff cut him off.

'Who gives a rats ass what you think!'

'Hell, we can't go up there,' Jenny questioned, 'can we?'

'Of course we can't,' Wally joined in, 'he want's to kill us all, I mean Sulkar, for Christ sakes?'

The more anyone said the more panicky they made each other. They were as much rattled by Quigley's call as anything else even though he had been on deck where they could see him during the attack on Debbie. They knew that, yet every fiber in each of their bodies told them to be afraid, and not only afraid of Sulkar. Voices began rising. Jenny articulated in a yelp what some of them now believed.

'He wants to eat us for God's sake.' She cried.

'Cook us first.'

'Oh, stop it, all of you!' Mary put her hands to her ears.

'Face facts, that smell on those nights, remember.'

'Two nights.'

'Three, I think.'

'Two, three,' Jeff said angrily, 'what's the goddamned difference!'

It was about to get completely out of hand.

'Let's try to stay calm,' Tommy said as though they were calm and of course they were not, 'first thing we have to decide is whether we go up now.'

'We can't,' Jeff said, 'we have to stay where we are, this way we've got 'em locked out.'

Spencer shook his head. 'We don't have them locked out, they have us locked in.'

'Why don't you just shut the hell up!'

'Why don't you!' Wally shouted at Jeff.

'Don't you see, Spencer's right,' Val declared, 'we can't stay down here forever.'

'But we have to plan,' Tommy answered, 'I know what that sounds like, but any plan is better than no plan. I think two or three of us should go up there.'

'We've been through that before.' Frank exclaimed.

'Yes but think about it,' Spencer said, 'maybe the captain doesn't know what happened last night, if it was just Sulkar on his own doing this stuff, how would he know?'

Some of them took a moment to think that over.

'Well, I for one,' Debbie declared, 'am not leaving here, not now anyway.'

That caused Jeff to explode. 'If it wasn't for you maybe none of this would have happened—greedy bitch!'

'Don't call me a bitch, asshole!'

The whole cabin was about to erupt into total chaos. But they stopped the yelling at each other instantly when Quigley called down again.

'Ahoy below!'

Tommy went back to the bottom of the companionway stairs and answered him.

'Okay, give us a couple of minutes.'

'Captain said all hands on deck.'

'We're talking it over.'

'Captain said—'

'We heard you, for Christ's sake!'

'Captain said get up here on deck!'

Jeff ran to the door and yelled. 'Fuck you!'

Others began to sound off.

'Tommy,' Val was barely able to make him hear her above a mounting clamor. 'Tommy—listen to me! Suspicion and fear is about to drive them crazy, we have to do something positive—now!'

Tommy recalled Val's earlier warning, "fear engenders anger, frustration produces indecision, inaction and self-doubt, finally all circling back to fear." He took a quick look around. He could easily read the fear and rising panic that covered every face. And the fear that Val had so rightly recognized as the danger that was perhaps becoming as great down here as the danger above. He decided and went to the bottom of the companionway.

'We're coming up!'

Tommy's head appeared through the companionway hatch, then he emerged to stand on the deck facing aft. Val and Spencer followed closely behind. Captain Burke was standing at his usual station in front of the wheel house. Quigley was at the helm. While Tommy kept his eyes locked on the captain, Spencer and Val looked around carefully but Sulkar was nowhere in sight. They approached cautiously and stopped, leaving a prudent distance between themselves and the captain.

'Well now, a good deal late in commencing the morning duties, don't you think?' The captain said in an even and oddly softer tone of voice.

'What do you expect, after what happened last night,' Tommy was careful not to speak loud or sound in the least forceful to match the captains seemingly non- belligerent manner.

'What do I expect?' Captain Burke measured the words but did not raise his voice, 'I expect, that every hand aboard this vessel will do his duty, at all times.'

Both his tone and demeanor were milder than at any time before and it caused them to wonder what he was up to.

'Every hand,' Val said, 'those of us that are left you mean,'

'Ah, yes, you refer of course, to those crew members who had to leave their duties.'

The softer attitude and affability was engendering a good deal of confusion in them, it was not what they had come to expect from him. They exchanged glances as they waited for the captain to continue. He turned his head so as to face the sea.

'Many members of crews of other vessels have had to leave their duties over these many years. Now see you here, boy, it is over with now, so let's have done with it. It is finished.'

'Over? . . . Finished?' Tommy said suspiciously while still keeping his voice in check. 'What's over . . . what's finished?'

The captain turned back to face them again.

'Over and done with, you have my word on it as captain of the vessel.' He looked away from them. 'The great sea, can be a cruel master. It is finished now.'

They stood watching him.

'What's he up to?' Spencer whispered in an aside to Tommy.

'We want to go home, now.' Val said forcefully.

'What do you say to that?' Tommy said.

The captain looked them over carefully before answering.

'Nothing more than you do your duty.' There seemed to be, in his tone, an effort to persuade. 'I'll get you all safe home, never fear.'

Tommy held up a hand to the captain indicating that they would talk it over. First, they moved a little back toward the companionway so as to be sure of what they were saying would not be overheard. They discussed the situation as it now stood and were completely perplexed by the captain's new attitude. He had been inflexible in every respect, now he was being close to agreeable. It was perhaps odd to think in the light of all that had happened that as far as they knew, he had never lied to them—but that is what Val was thinking. He had no reason to lie. If they asked him something he would simply ignore them. He would not be evasive he would just not answer at all. He told them what to do and that's all. They had no proof of lies anyway. In fact if they thought about it, he had not told them very much at all. The three of them that now faced the captain knew the difference between telling a lie and failing to tell the truth, that could be called lying by default. The truth, or lying by omission is essentially a fine distinction anyway. Nothing that he had ever said before had confused them as much as what the captain was now saying.

Here was a entirely different captain telling them that everything would be all right, that he would see to it that they got home safely. He had never said anything like that before. It was either an outright lie or the truth. It was as simple as that. He had never treated them as anything but subordinates and to his way, it was not required that he take them into his confidence at any time. Now he was doing the opposite of everything he had

155

done from the beginning of the voyage. There had to be a lot more to all this than they could conceive at this moment.

But did they have anything to bargain with? And what were they bargaining for anyway? Their lives? On the other hand he had just told them what they had to bargain with—their duty. They needed him to get back to land and he needed them to sail the ship. That is what he had said on their second day on board—a crew to sail the vessel—that was the bargain. After a few more whispered words in a tight exchange while staying alert for trouble it was agreed what they would do. Tommy spoke again for all of them, those on deck and the others waiting below.

'You say you will take us back, right?'

'That is so.'

'Do we have your word on that?'

'All I ask is that you return to duty. We need each other to sail the vessel, what has happened is past. Best forgotten. It is done with now.'

'Done with?' Tommy and Val said it at almost the same time. 'What is done with?'

'It is,' he seemed to drift a little, 'it is done.'

The vagueness of the words were so puzzling that Tommy glanced at Spencer for some help in understanding but he shook his head indicating that he didn't know either. Val was as baffled as Spencer.

Then the captain surprised them again, his face softened.

'Now look you here, all will be well.'

'Captain,' Tommy wanted a more definitive answer, 'do you give us your word that you will sail for land now?'

'For land?'

'That's right, sail for the land, your word,' he said insistently, 'captain, do we have your word?'

The captain angled his body slightly toward the port side of the ship and he stared at the sea for a long time. Then he turned back to face them square on. Even so, he hesitated before giving them a mumbling, incoherent answer.

'The ship must be, must be at all times, ah . . .' His voice trailed off.

Tommy figured that it was the best they could do. Whether that was a yes or no Tommy had no idea. Spencer shrugged and, then nodded. And Val placed her arm though Tommy's as her way of saying what Tommy did was okay with her but she too confronted the captain.

'You do know what happened last night?' Val asserted in the same manner that Tommy had spoken, firm—not angry, 'you know about that don't you?'

'Last night?' The captain seemed as though he wasn't looking at them, more looking through them, to the sea.

'Ah,' he murmured, 'last night?'

'Sulkar, captain,' Tommy said, 'you know about Sulkar and what happened last night?'

'Sulkar?'

'He attacked one of the crew, you know that don't you?'

'Sulkar? Last night.'

They couldn't be sure if his words were an affirmation or a question. He appeared to be drifting again. It seemed that he could not take in, or was unable to grasp what they were saying. They looked at each other and wondered if he knew or not, he was giving no indication either way. He looked as though he was thinking yet his eyes peered into some far off place at the same time. So disconcerting was his gaze that Spencer turned for a few seconds to see if there was anything out there, but he could see nothing but the vast, empty ocean. A full minute passed before he spoke again. And when he did it was as though he had resolved something in his mind.

'Sulkar . . . yes, Sulkar will be punished.'

Fifteen

'Take up the slack!'

The ship was laying quite still riding on a sea anchor that Quigley had set out during the pre dawn hours, the anchor held the ship from drifting and stabilized her against a nonchalant westerly current that passed around and under her.

'Tighten it up the slack on them lines now, good—stand by.'

The whole crew, even those who would normally be working below at that time, had been called and were now shuffling around on the middle deck where Quigley had told them to stand.

At that time they did not know why but each of them was holding a long rope that extended to the very end of the ship and out over the stern railing. There were two ropes actually that would ultimately join up to serve the same purpose. The captain was at his usual station, in front of the wheel house. Quigley was standing to on the forward deck close to the bow. The crew was separated, half of them on the port side of the deck, the rest, on the starboard side. They stood in two equal lines, facing each other. The ropes were laying fore and aft from the stern to where they were stationed on the middle deck.

Quigley had instructed them when they came on deck that they were, when the order was given, to haul on the ropes with an even strain as they moved along the deck. He had explained, if one man were opposite another crew member on the other rope you should remain opposite the same person as they both hauled away toward the bow of the ship. Other than that, he had told them nothing. They had no idea of what was going on. Then they saw him. The giant Sulkar was bound with a another set of ropes. Ropes that circled his massive arms and chest and ended up around his back where his hands were securely tied behind him, his legs however, were free of any binding. His enormous body was supported between two of the bowsprit lines. He seemed to be somewhat disinterested in the proceedings as though what was about to happen was going to happen to someone else. But he knew exactly what was going to happen. Sulkar had his eyes fixed on the captain but he revealed no expression of fear.

When the captain gave the order the Bos'n would be dragged off the bow and into the sea to be pulled along the length of the ship under the keel and hauled up at the other end over the stern. The operation would, in all likelihood—kill him. The jagged crustaceans on the bottom of the ship would cut his body to pieces and if that did not kill him, he would either drown or bleed to death.

With a nod from the captain, Quigley attached the ropes to those that held the Bos'n so securely. Now it was set. Sulkar was coupled to the two ropes that were running under the ship and up over the stern, one for the port side and the other for starboard. The end of the ropes were that which the crew were now holding. So that when they hauled on them they would be pulling away from the stern and toward the bow. When he had been given a signal from Quigley that the tying off had been completed, the captain nodded and Quigley shouted.

'Attention on deck!'

Captain Burke began reading from a book.

'Article 72. Any mariner, seaman or officer, while at sea, strikes or in any way injures another mariner, seaman or officer shall suffer the penalty as prescribed by the law of the sea. Such punishment as decreed in the article is that any such, Mariner, Seaman or Officer shall be—' he looked up from the page for a moment to stare at Sulkar, 'shall be keel hauled.'

He snapped the book shut and gripped it firmly in his hand before calling to Quigley at the bow end of the ship.

'Mister Quigley?'

'Ready captain.'

'Very well.'

'Stand by now,' Quigley instructed the crew, 'be ready to haul on the lines when the captain gives the order.'

Now they knew. Now they realized that Sulkar was about to be dragged along the full length of the ship's bottom. Captain Burke raised the book high in the air and held it there for what seemed like a very long time then suddenly, he let the hand drop.

'Haul away! Haul away!' Quigley shouted.

They began hauling on the ropes as they moved forward along the deck. Sulkar was plucked violently off the bowsprit lines, that until then had supported his body, and plummeted into the sea. Quigley ran to stand between the two lines as they moved forward along the deck hauling Sulkar along the keel of the ship. The crew were horrified when they understood what was happening and more so now that they realized they were part of it. But they also comprehended very quickly that if they didn't pull hard, Sulkar was surely doomed. The bos'un was generally disliked but none of them could conceive of such a punishment. It was surely a death sentence and summary execution.

'Pull—all of you—pull! It's his only chance!' Quigley shouted at them, 'the faster he comes along down there the more chance he has!'

Sulkar went into the water, plunging deeper than the bow at first then began to rise up to the bottom of the ship as the ropes became taught. He used his feet and legs to keep himself off the keel for as long as he could but that only lasted for a few seconds before his first encounter with massive crustaceans that covered the bottom of the ship from stem to stern. Deep wounds were inflicted from the moment his body came into contact with the ship. Blood began to spurt immediately from his back, his chest, legs and arms. Small pieces of flesh were torn from almost every part of his body and each separated part began a slow journey— floating up to the surface. Along with a chunk of flesh with trailing membrane, one of Sulkar's eyes was ripped neatly from it's socket and blood squirted from the gaping hole it left in his undersized head. Forced out by the pressure in his scull, the eye shot out and away from him as though fired from the barrel of a gun. A passing shark snapped it up quickly and proceeded to follow Sulkar in his deadly tumble hoping for other such tasty morsels.

'Pull!' Quigley shouted, 'pull damn you! Pull!' Quigley shouted frantically.

More than half way along the keel Sulkar's head struck a hard grouping of heavy shell that inflicted a gash in the back of his head that caused him to lose consciousness.

'Pull!'

It took every once of strength from each of them to drag Sulkar from the water when he broke the surface at the stern of the ship. What was left of the bos'un was finally hauled up over the stern railings and onto the deck. Most of them had to look away from the horror that was once a man. Some though, found it an impossible task to turn away. Almost as though the sight was so incredibly hideous that it demanded that they see it no matter what the consequences to their mind and body might be.

Sulkar was not dead. Remarkably, at least for now, he had survived the most gruesome of punishments. The captain watched as he was taken by Quigley and six of the others on a strip of canvas that amounted to no more than a crude stretcher. Leaving a trail or blood along the deck, he was carried, at times dragged for he was still a formidable weight, to the forward superstructure and though the hatch to his quarters. Quigley dismissed the six and closed the door quickly behind them. The sight of the fearful wounds left them in no doubt that Sulkar would be dead within a short time. Some of them went straight to the railings to puke over the side. Most though, hurried back to the companionway hatch in befuddled shock avoiding while doing so, the trail of blood and small pieces of flesh that were now slowly running from the deck to the scuppers and finally over the side into the beautiful, clear blue ocean.

Sixteen

'I still say we're nuts to be doing this.'

It had been decided that the only thing they could do for now was to obey the captain's orders. That at least would keep the ship moving. They thought if they were heading somewhere, anywhere, they had a chance of reaching a port or an island, even the deserted island that some had suggested would be okay.

'We should do what I wanted,' Jeff repeated, 'take over.' Few were paying him any attention. But he continued the carping that all were sick of hearing. 'What the hell, we'd have to hit land sooner or later, like you said, just head east or west and keep going till we get some place, it doesn't matter, north, south, east or west.'

'Or all at the same time.' Spencer retorted, 'Don't you get it? We can't do anything until we know where we are and we can't know that until we get another look at those charts.'

'He's right,' Tommy said, 'we have to know where we are, before we can take any action.'

'I've been working on a plan that could work once we know, even approximately where we—'

'I have a plan for you,' Jeff told Spencer, 'write it down and shove it approximately up your ass.'

'That just doesn't help anything Jeff.' Val chided him. 'If we stay together, like we've been doing, stay safe, he has to head for land sooner or—'

'Okay, okay,' Jeff stopped her, 'but when you want to rush them, I'm ready. With Sulkar out of the way, it should be easy.'

They were on deck working but the workload was so nonessential that it really didn't matter whether they did it or not. The ship was under light sail, the sea was relatively placid with a rolling swell in a north to south current and when there was a change of course, two or three simple adjustments to the sailing rig was all that was required. Until the next course variation, they had little to do. Even so, Quigley told them what to do and then went almost immediately to do it himself. It seemed that with someone at the helm and given the prevailing fair conditions, the ship could probably be run by Quigley and two or three of them. Naturally, that could change if the weather blew up.

As for Quigley, he seemed to be in some kind of daze since the keel hauling of the Bos'n. The fact was that without him the punishment could not have taken place. There was also no doubt that had Sulkar resisted there was no way that Quigley could have overpowered him. It seemed absurd but there was no question that Sulkar himself had abetted in his own near execution. Even though he was an essential part of it, the punishment that the bos'un had endured appeared to have affected Quigley in a strange way. Perhaps he was afraid that the same thing could happen to himself or, maybe he feared revenge. For Sulkar was, unbelievably, still alive. He had not appeared on deck and Quigley had told them nothing but that the bos'un was not dead.

'That's what we should do,' Jeff went on while keeping an eye out for Quigley, 'take over, you know it's the only thing we can do, don't you see?'

Tommy frowned and shook his head, Val was about to say something when Spencer spoke quietly.

'It may come to that, anyway.'

'What?' Tommy exclaimed.

'That's right, it may come to that.'

'Boy that's a switch.'

'I know, but think of it this way,' Spencer went on as some of the others joined them. 'He is crazy, right?'

'There's no doubt about that now is there Val?,' Tommy said, 'not after what he did to Sulkar.'

'Yes,' Val said cautiously, 'I believe he could be crazy, crazy being a generic term. He's now presenting signs of schizophrenia as well as whatever else is psychosomatically wrong with him.'

'Does that mean he's a mental fruit cake?' Tommy asked her.

'Yes' Val declared, 'he's a Freudian delight, he's crawling with clues but that doesn't necessarily mean he's insane.'

'In addition to that, you want to know something?' Spencer proclaimed, 'keel hauling was outlawed over two hundred years ago, in seventeen seventy nine I believe, more than two hundred years ago.'

'How do you know that?' Jeff asked.

'I read it somewhere,'

'Ask a stupid question,' Val said.

'Anyway,' Spencer said, 'there is no doubt now that it is what I thought all along, Val.'

'What?'

'Think about the way he spoke to us when we were refusing to work. Old English, that's how he spoke, in old English,'

'Yeah, he did.' Tommy affirmed.

'So,' Spencer rationalized, 'he's either living in another century or . . .'

'Or?'

'Or . . . or he's from another century.'

Throughout the day they tried to come to a decision upon which everyone could agree. And again, there was a great deal of useless wrangling. They did find a consensus however, that they were in a stronger position to do what Jeff wanted now that Sulkar was not part of the problem. Another thing, some of them thought now that the captain had punished Sulkar because he knew for sure that he was the one who had killed Alex and Beth. Along with that, a couple of them at least, thought that there was some good in the captain for doing what he did to Sulkar. It appeared as though he was unyielding in metering out harsh justice to the perpetrator. Because of these two things most of them felt a little safer. If the captain believed Sulkar was the murderer, they were more than willing to believe it too.

But now there was a feeling that there should be one last effort to get the captain to head for land. If he didn't do so, then they were left no option but to try to take over the ship. Sentiments for this course of action were running stronger. Jeff had gathered a lot more support for his idea since the Bos'n was no longer a threat, especially from the Australians but they were by no means the only ones in favor of such action.

'Okay,' Tommy was saying, 'what we got from the charts didn't help much. We should try for another look at them, but say we can't?'

Jeff was more sure of himself than the others and he was never one to hold his tongue.

'Yeah, what then? You all know what I think.'

'Then,' Spencer said, 'we'd have to guessestimate what would be the nearest land, and head for it, I guess.'

'That's maybe one guess too many,' Tommy said, 'no doubt about it, we have to see the charts again.'

'Yes,' Val agreed, 'that's exactly what we have to do.'

'All right then,' Tommy said, 'we seem to be headed in a westerly direction at this time, right?'

There was a lot of nodding and a general agreement that the ship was heading west right now, but—

'That's right,' Wally cut in, 'and that would be heading us back toward Australia,'

'Yeah, back there,' Jeff agreed, 'that's the idea right?'

Spencer was shaking his head. Jeff didn't like that.

'What?' He said jabbing his palms up at Spencer.

'So far as it goes, okay.' Spencer said thoughtfully. 'But think about it. Let's assume for a moment that Sulkar was not the one who did it, say he had nothing to do with it?'

'But he was.'

'Or, not the only one if you like, say the captain was in on it, okay?'

'Assuming that, then what?' Tommy wanted to know more.

'Then,' Spencer went on with more emphasis on certain words, 'how can he expect to get away with it? If he brings us back to a port, any port, once we report it, he's bound to get caught.'

'He's right, Spencer's right,' Jenny asserted, 'I always thought that if he takes us back he'll get caught,'

'That is if it wasn't Sulkar that did everything,' Wally cut in, 'I mean, who threw Alex and Beth over the side.'

'We know,' Tommy said, 'for sure it was Sulkar that grabbed Debbie, we know that for certain,'

'Do we?' Spencer said. 'I'm still not sure'

They looked at him.

'Of course it was Sulkar,' Jenny asserted, 'that's the only thing that we can be sure of, Tommy saw him.'

Jeff spoke up articulating what the rest of them believed.

'The captain must have thought so, look what he did to Sulkar for doing it?'

'And Sulkar took the punishment as though he was guilty didn't he?' Debbie said, 'I mean, because he was guilty.'

'Listen to me,' Val spoke up, 'if the Captain told Sulkar to jump into the water and tow the ship across the Pacific, he would have jumped in.'

'Why?'

'Because he is under the captain's control, so is Quigley.'

'But that would—'

'Look,' Val went on emphatically, 'I can give you a lot of what it means psychologically and psychopathically which we don't have time for — just believe me, he has that kind of power. And it's not that unusual for one person to have complete psychological control of another, many dictators for instance—and they had it over millions of people.'

'You mean hypnosis,' Jenny said, 'or something like that?'

'No, not that,' Val said, 'there are other forms of control . . . right now he has physical control of us. Physical, not the psychological control that he has over Sulkar and Quigley. He has control of the ship—therefore—us. However, the control he has over Quigley and Sulkar that's different and it can't be just because of their sense of duty—there's got to be more to it than that.'

They fell silent for a moment then Spencer took up his argument again.

'Let's say one of them might be some kind of crazy. And let's say one of them is the killer and that he is a schitzo, he could kill and then he could go for a long time before the urge to kill again takes over—or it could happen again tonight.'

'Even if that's not true,' Val cut in, 'we've got to stay together like we've been doing, we just don't know what could happen.'

'Yes, that's the best for right now,' Tommy agreed, 'but we have to be ready for anything.'

'Ready,' Jeff said emphatically, 'I'm sure as hell ready!'

'How about this then?' Tommy suggested, 'we insist that he head, fast as possible, back to Australia, right?'

'We've done that before,' Jeff claimed, 'and it didn't work.'

'This time it has to be a demand,' Tommy told them, 'but we have to be prepared to back it up.'

Most of them thought this was a good idea.

'Right!'

'Absolutely!'

'And,' Spencer said, 'we sneak another look at the maps and charts if we can?'

More agreement.

'That's it!'

'Our best chance!'

'And then,' Tommy went on, 'if none of that is any good, if the charts are not there or something, then—'

'Yeah, then what?'

'Why then,' Jeff cut in, 'at the first opportunity, we rush him. Okay?'

'Yes, definitely,'

'Sure, that's it.'

'Why not,'

'What have we got to lose?'

And on this, there was for the first time, absolute agreement.

'All right, just be on the alert at all times,' Tommy warned them, 'and we don't know what Quigley will do. And don't forget, he might not be totally crazy.'

'Nuts is nuts!' Jeff said.

'You should know.' Debbie injected the only note of levity. Maybe it was something they needed, in any case it prompted one or two laughs, timorous, nervous laughter but it took the edge off but only a little and for a few brief moments because then they heard Quigley.

'Those hands doin' navigation, report to the wheelhouse right away!' Quigley shouted from the deck, his squeaky voice rattling down the aft companionway.

'Ah ha!' Spencer declared, 'this is our chance to see those charts.'

'See, Tommy, he's acting normal again,' Val said, 'just as though nothing has happened. Schizophrenia's can be two entirely different people sharing the same body and brain, right now, he's normal.'

'Normal? If you're right, Val, and he is two different people, I think both of them are insane.'

'Yes,' Val answered seriously, 'that's very possible.'

'Let's go,' Tommy said, 'but watch out, we'll try to see the charts. If we can find out where we are it has to help. For Christ's sake, stay with a least one other person. Everybody, one buddy at least, okay?'

'Yes,' Val enforced, 'no one is to be alone.'

'Absolutely.' Spencer said as he headed for the companionway.

'Here Tommy,' Jeff took him aside a little, 'take this knife.'

'How about you?'

Jeff pulled a marlin spike from his belt. 'That's okay, I got this.'

'All right, Jeff, then how about you have everyone arm themselves with whatever they can, just in case, okay?'

'Now you're talking, buddy, now you're talking!'

Quigley called down again,

'The captains waiting!'

Seventeen

'All clear?'

Mid afternoon found them assembled in the main cabin, some were leaning over the mess table, as were Tommy and Val, and others were standing with their backs to one of the bulkheads either the one by the galley or forward or aft of the cabin. But they immediately crowded around when Tommy spread a large sheet of paper on the table. There was a swelling air of expectancy. One of the them stood guard at each of the entrances, both lookouts nodded back to Tommy's questioning look, neither Quigley or the captain were near any of the entrances that lead down to the lower deck. Wally made a quick run down the steps of the companionway after checking on what was happening above.

'It's okay, the captain's in the wheel house and Quigley's up on the high forward deck.'

'On my deck?' Jeff said, 'the Larrikin's deck, the asshole!'

'All right, let's get started,' Tommy said in a low voice, deeming it prudent to be careful regardless. 'Okay here it is, this is what we found out today from the charts. To begin with though, remember when we started out we thought we would always be fairly near the Australian coast, right?'

'Australia,' there was nostalgia in Wally's tone as he lowered his voice, 'that seems like a long time ago.'

'It sure does.' Frank agreed, 'Who knew we wouldn't be just goofing up and down the coast,'

'And diving the reef.' Jack remarked wistfully.

'We know all that,' Jeff said querulously. 'What I want to know is where we are now?'

'Right! Where are we?' Jenny also impatient. 'Where?'

'Well see, here's the thing,' Tommy looked around the table. 'We're still not certain.' He said candidly.

'Beautiful, friggin' beautiful.' Jeff bellyached what most of them felt.

'But, we have a rough idea now,' Tommy stopped Jeff before they became embroiled in another distracting wrangle, 'now take a look. We were sailing east for the first part of the trip.'

The large square of paper had a map traced on it. Tommy tracked the lines of their voyage.

'Say, for some time we went like this, right? For several days, and —'

They crowded closer around the table trying to get a good look at the chart that Tommy had laid out.

'And nights.' Spencer added.

'Well yes,' Tommy agreed, 'then we began to tack and change directions all the time, that confused us a lot more than anything else, but after seeing what we think is the captain's main chart and the other one, we think we might, see here? Like this by tracing over the two maps and sort of making them into one chart on it's own, we might be able to—'

'Extrapolate,' Spencer cut in again.

'Yes, extrapolate.' Tommy traced the zigzag course on the paper after checking a lot of numbers that Spencer had written in a small notebook. 'Now see, after the truce we sailed to here that was west, and that was at the point when he was supposed to take us back, like he said he would, when he gave us his word.'

'Well, that's good, isn't it?' Jeff offered.

'It would be but for one thing.' Spencer told him.

'Yeah, what's that?'

'Wait a sec.' Tommy said.

They watched silently as Tommy pointed to another set of squiggled lines that indicated the multiple tacking that were part of the course changes the ship had made. So many lines that they began to cover the whole sheet of paper.

'See,' Tommy leaned over the chart, 'he tacked and changed so much and at a fairly slow speed. And another thing, he went for long stretches with a whole heap of changes, that it is very hard to figure it out for a while. But we think we may have something now.'

'So, where are we?

'Hold on, Jeff,'

They watched carefully what Tommy was doing but it was impossible to make any sense out of it. The whole sheet now looked like a mass of lines going every which way and crossing and re-crossing one another.

'Now if we can disregard all the changes and tacking and the rest of these things, like this.'

Tommy made a straight line, a line like none of the others on the paper, longer and bolder. A line that cut right through the tacking and course changes and all the other lines. He stopped at a certain point.

'See, it appears for most of the time, the day light hours that is, even given the taking and so on, we sailed a heading of two hundred and seventy degrees, due west, like this.'

Tommy made another straight line but this one, a more distinct heavy black line. 'Then, at night he changed course, twice in fact, the first change, was like here.' Again he etched a bolder line and again, cutting through all of the other lines. 'Now you can see here, south, southeast, on one hundred and fifty five degrees then . . .'

He made another mark.

'. . . the third course, as near as we can figure, was north east on zero four five degrees, like this.' He pushed the marker through to the other side of the page where it joined with the one he had just made.

Silence.

They could all see that Tommy had made three perfect lines that ran through all the confusing zigzags. Three heavy black lines that joined each other.

'We're not going anywhere,' Jenny said, her eyes wide, her voice dropped to a whisper, 'he's not taking us home, we're not going anywhere, like the name of this freaking boat, nowhere.' Her voice was so soft that it was hard to believe that she really understood the significance of the lines. But she did, they all did. Laura didn't scream, it was more like an inhaled sigh. A scream would have made everyone jump. This was worse than any scream.

'Circles, the son-of-a-bitch is taking us around in circles!' Jeff barked.

'Well, a triangle actually,' Spencer told him, 'but it's pretty much the same thing, and he's been repeating it over and over, but during the day when we are on deck, it always appeared that we were sailing west which is what we wanted, back to the coast, back to Cape Upstart.'

'Then at night,' Tommy said, 'he changed to the other two courses of the triangle. And by the time we came on deck in the morning, we'd be sailing with the sun behind us, obviously going west. He would have resumed the first course, which is back on two hundred and seventy degrees, that is due west. We don't know how many times, but it seems sure that he has been repeating it from the time we got to a certain point in the Pacific Ocean.'

'It looks like he wants to stay in this area, for some reason.' Spencer said.

'So he can kill us all.' Mary said, her voice no more than a soft breath.

Spencer looked directly at the map then said offhandedly as though it was simply a matter of fact.

'Yes, possibly, but then he could kill us anywhere. There has to be another reason.'

'So, where is this triangle, Tommy?' Mary asked.

'As near as we can figure about . . . . here, two or three hundred miles south west of the Fijian Islands.'

There was another silence. Some of them flopped down on the deck dejectedly. Jenny asked the question on everyone's mind. 'What do we do now?'

'We have no choice.' Spencer told her.

'You mean, we just wait to get killed?' Jenny said, alarm in her voice.

'No!' Tommy declared, 'we have to take the ship!'

'All right!' Jeff shouted, 'when?'

'As soon as he comes on deck tomorrow morning that will give us is time tonight to prepare—to get everything ready.'

'Man, I'm ready right now!'

'Tommy, do you think we can sail her to those islands,' Val said, trying to keep the uneasiness out of her voice. 'I mean one of the Islands?'

'Val, he doesn't intend to take us back.'

'Take over,' Jeff said, 'yes!'

'What are we going to do in the morning?' Frank wanted to know.

'We have to overpower the captain and Quigley,' Spencer said, 'then tie them up, and lock them up, then sail the ship to the nearest Island,'

'Tahiti or New Caledonia,' Tommy said, 'or maybe if we are still close, Fiji.'

'Yeah, it could be one of the Fijian Group of Islands,' Spencer said, 'depends on the ship's position in the morning, wherever is closest.'

'Okay,' Wally said, 'say we can sail her but—'

'Tommy can navigate,' Spencer said anticipating the question.

Tommy shook his head. 'I don't know, maybe.'

'Everyone will have to help tomorrow,' Val said glancing gingerly around the table, 'we'll all have something to do.'

'Yes, tonight we have to figure out the exact plan,' Spencer declared, 'and we have got to stick to it, okay?'

Jeff nodded his agreement with Spencer—the first time he'd ever done that.

'I'm ready,' he said punching a fist into his palm, 'man am I ready!'

Some of the others joined in with varying degrees of enthusiasm, spirits were on the rise. But Tommy did not join in the high five's that many of them were doing or any of the other brazen exhibitions of game on behavior they were presenting.

Instead, he stared at the map frowning. It was a big ship to sail. Viewing it from the other perspective, it was a small ship on a very big ocean. The frown deepened. Val took a firm grip on his hand, he turned to face her. She looked into his eyes. She didn't have to say anything.

Eighteen

'He's never this late.'

There had been no extra watches assigned to them. Quigley called them to the deck late, long after the tolling of eight bells and they began what appeared to be another light work day, a lazy setting so far as any schedule of work was concerned, nothing of any real consequence was ordered by the first mate. Quigley was still Quigley but a significantly different man, more subdued, he was not the overbearing, sometimes half-witted giggling first mate of before. Two things surprised them. Through a light but dismal sea haze they could see that the ship was only now shifting to the west, with the sun rising fast into the sky astern of them. And two, Sulkar was on deck! He looked like a corpse that was breathing and should not be.

For some time there had been no weather to speak of. The seas had remained morosely calm for the last several days as though in deep slumber. Through the haze, banks of high clouds were visible to the north, fluffy and white offering no menace. To the south, east and west—nothing. And there was no real work to do. That was perhaps ideal for their purposes which would begin, if it all went according to plan, after the captain appeared on deck.

The plan had been checked and double checked. Then gone over in detail again. They were ready.

They had not, of course, taken into account the fact that Sulkar might be there. Everyone thought he was dead or at the least so near death that he would be no threat to their plans. Even now, when looking at what was in essence, a dead man, they decided to leave him out of the equation. It was difficult for them to accept that he was still a live being. There was a gaping hole in his head where his right eye used to be and the scores of unhealed open wounds from the razor sharp barnacles and other crustaceans that he had encountered on his journey along the bottom of the ship were oozing blood. Darker than the normal red, tenebrous blood leached from almost every part of his shattered body. He was a cadaver looking for a place to lie down, dry out and disappear into dust.

Tommy, Val and the rest of them looked at his mangled, blood-clotted body as they came up from below. He was on the deck on the very hindmost part of the ship, the gunwale of the after deck. He sat at an eccentric angle, his back resting against a port side bollard and what was left of his legs extended grotesquely and looked as though they were not really part of his body anymore. Sulkar was almost out of sight being behind the aft superstructure and the wheel house in front of that. With his one eye half closed he was a gruesome monstrosity that they took one glance at then looked away quickly. Even so, considering all aspects of the plan, Tommy considered reassigning two or three of the crew to watch him when they began the take over but in the end he decided not to do so.

As they came on deck Quigley was in the process of turning the ship toward the west, which would take her off the north westerly slice of the triangle. That told them that the captain was sticking to his courses without alteration. If they needed one— that was the clincher that confirmed for them that they had to carry out their plan. That the captain was not going to head back to Australia—that he was not going to let them get off the ship. That he was going to triangulate the ship around this dreary stretch of ocean.

Quigley lashed the wheel down to let the ship wallow along at so easy a pace that she was barely making way, perhaps even drifting. It didn't seem to matter to him, where the ship was headed. This was of course all very strange to them given the precise nature of what the voyage had been up to that point.

As a group they were now, more than ever, determined to carry out the take-over no matter what. Quigley left the wheelhouse and moved about the deck distractedly. He gave a few orders which, considering the situation from their point of view, didn't really matter that much. Other than that, he spoke to no one and seemed in the same kind of stupor that he was after the keel hauling of what once was the giant Sulkar and who was now nothing but a mountain of cleaved flesh in a bundle of bloody rags looking for a place to die.

The crew went about the things Quigley told them to do in an orderly but perfunctory manner. There was none of the snap to it of the preceding days. It was a strange ambiance, or to be more precise, no discernible ambiance. The life had been taken out of Quigley it seemed, almost as much as Sulkar. As though the life had been taken out of the ship itself. That was the environment aboard the *Erehwon* they encountered that day and, even though the heat was oppressive, many of them felt a cold shiver running down their spine.

Tommy cast a watchful eye out for the captain, but he had yet to appear on deck. They thought it best that they were doing the tasks that Quigley ordered them to do. Those duties anyway had become routine and pretty much second nature to them, tightening off any slack lines and adjusting the almost purposeless sail settings. Tommy wanted Quigley to get the impression that they thought everything was normal. So they went about their duties very much as usual, light and meaningless though those duties were because if the take-over worked out they would soon be turning the ship to the North and making all speed toward Fiji or Tahiti or any one of the islands that lay to the north.

'It has to be something, he's never been this late. Something's up.'

'Nothing's up, Jeff.' Tommy told him. 'He'll be here, you got everything straight?'

'Don't worry about me, I'm the one who volunteered.'

'Just remember, if we have trouble tying him up, what we said, okay?'

Jeff pulled the marlin spike half way out of his belt.

'Yeah sure, but you guys be ready with the rope to tie him up or I'll—'

Tommy nodded.

'Val, you all set?'

'Yes, all set.'

'Good, just have your people ready to handle Quigley, we have to stop him if he tries anything, I don't know what he'll do so just be ready to tie him up as quickly as you can, got it?'

'There are six of us for that assignment, we shouldn't have any trouble. Jeff has the tough job.' Val replied directing the last few words to Jeff.

'Don't worry about me, dude.'

'Okay then,' Tommy said, 'better get into position, he should be coming on deck anytime now.'

'Right.'

Jeff moved off to his assigned station near the stern of the ship behind the wheel house hatchway, Tommy and Spencer followed him and the others who were to handle the captain, moved closer. Everyone, Jeff especially, avoided looking at Sulkar laying at the end of the ship.

'Come along now,' Quigley muttered weakly, mechanically, as though by habit alone. Gone the vitality of his high pitched commands of days before. He spoke in what was now nothing more than a mumble—said without looking at any of them—as though he was speaking to no one, trance-like and detached, 'bend to it.' he muttered.

They worked, or appeared to be working, at their various jobs but many eyes were trained on the hatchway through which the captain would emerge. They knew that he would then either proceed to the wheelhouse or else in front of it if he was going to issue any orders. Jeff moved to, and stood in a position between the aft superstructure and the wheel house. Captain Burke would have to pass him if he were going to the deck or the wheelhouse. At that moment Quigley ordered Wally to take the helm. Wally looked at Tommy who nodded that he should do as Quigley had said. Wally went into the wheelhouse and took the helm. He called to Quigley,

'Is it steady as she goes?'

No answer.

'Is it steady as she goes? . . . Mister Quigley.'
Quigley nodded, 'Ah, steady as she goes.'

They waited. It seemed a long time for Jeff but in reality, it was not more than a few minutes before there was a sound from the hatch. With an incredibly loud clatter the latch snapped upward and the door opened suddenly. Even though they were expecting just that, it was a jolt when the door swung open and banged against the superstructure. The captain emerged.

They had resolved not to make one last appeal to the captain to return to Australia even though the proposal had been made by some of them. The time for talking had passed they had ultimately agreed. If they did make a last effort it might only put him on the alert, perhaps warning him of what was going to happen. They had decided it was risky, perhaps dangerous. They would do what they had to do and they would do it right from the start. Once the captain and Quigley were securely under their control they would carry out the rest of the plan. Tommy and the others had the ropes in their hands at the ready trying to look as though they were just going about their duties as usual.

Captain Burke walked quickly onto the deck and began making his way to his customary position in front of the wheelhouse. Jeff followed along behind, getting closer with each step. The captain moved along fast and was about to pass by the wheelhouse doorway when he turned abruptly to face Jeff full on. A sweat quickly broke out on Jeff's face. He stood as though nailed to the deck for what seemed like a very long time receiving the captain's stare. He was very aware of the marlin spike gripped tightly in his hand but if the captain thought there was anything unusual about that, he made no sign. Just as abruptly, the captain turned away, making his way along the deck. Then he stopped again. He changed his mind and turned to go into the wheelhouse.

'Open the hatch, boy.' He said to Jeff.

Jeff swallowed hard before he was able to answer in what was not anything like his normal voice.

'Yes sir.'

Jeff opened the hatch and the captain was about to enter but stopped again. He lifted a chart from his canvas jacket pocket and looked at it. At that moment, his head bent forward. The captain was right in front of Jeff—there would never be a better opportunity. The others that were close by held their breath as they waited for Jeff to make his move which would signal the rest of them into action. He appeared to raise the marlin spike. Wally, at the wheel—his eyes opened wide staring past the captain. He could see that Jeff that was about to do it and inched a little closer to the door while at the same time holding the wheel steady. Jeff was plainly sweating now. The captain was looking at the chart that he held in his slightly outstretched hands, Jeff was almost directly behind him. He raised the marlin spike high in the air then as the captain moved a little to his right, he lowered it. Everyone, with the exception of Quigley who was turned the other way, was watching now. The club ascended again higher and higher but still Jeff did not yet bring it down.

'Do it! For Christ's sake, do it, do it!' Tommy said under his breath.

'Hit him!' Wally whispered to no one but himself.

One after another, the crew became as hunters waiting for the blow to fall. Still Jeff did not seem to be able to bring the club down.

Three things happened at almost the same instant. Quigley turned and immediately realized what was about to happen. He shouted.

'Captain!'

Captain Burke looked up sharply, alert. Too late. Jeff was in the act of striking and the others were now running forward with the ropes. The marlin spike was about to descend but at that precise moment Sulkar, who had come up behind Jeff unnoticed, pushed him aside and bought a hatchet down on the captains head.

'Captain!' Quigley shouted again.

Jeff was shoved out of the way and an axe had come crashing down onto the captain's head. The blow was delivered by Sulkar with all the strength that was left in his mangled body. The captain was at the point of turning around in reaction to Quigley's warning and the turn had saved him from the full force of the blow. Even so, a deep gash was opened across the top of his scull, extending all the way down to the right ear.

Blood, spurting at first, began to flow freely down his face and neck. Jeff, even though pushed out of the way by Sulkar, received a profuse splattering of the captain's blood. With one hand on the door frame, the captain, although seriously wounded, was able to lurch all the way into the wheelhouse. And with his powerful left hand he grabbed Wally and flung him bodily to the other side of the wheelhouse knocking him out cold. Even though the others who were assigned to the task of tying up Quigley—with the ropes at the ready—no one had moved on him. There seemed to be no need, Quigley was just standing there, apparently stunned into complete immobility.

Nineteen

It had all happened so fast and nothing had worked out the way they had planned it. As Jeff was about to strike, Tommy had rushed forward with the rope ready to tie the captain up but Sulkar's action had botched this attempt. And worse, even though badly wounded, the captain was able to see what they were attempting to do. The take-over had not only failed, it was now exposed. The captain was wounded but not secured, not tied up and Wally was in the wheelhouse with him. Then something else happened that they had not anticipated, the captain pulled a gun from the pocket of his heavy sea coat.

'So you'd take my ship, would you?' Captain Burke shouted at them through the open side window of the wheel house. He took the large caliber revolver and pointed it at those on the other side of the wheelhouse door. Jeff was the closest and behind him, Tommy and Spencer. They backed away toward the others who were standing further along the deck as he leveled the gun at them.

'Mutiny is it?' the captain yelled, 'you should have looked to the sky first.'

From out of what was, moments before, a perfectly calm sea, a wave broke over the side of the ship throwing a spray around the wheelhouse obscuring the view of those on the deck. And then another wave. At the same time Wally was coming to. He was still a little groggy but he had no trouble seeing the gun pointed at his head. The captain stared menacingly at him for long seconds. His black eyes held steady on Wally who was by then getting to his feet and could do nothing but wait for the bullet that would shatter his brain. The captain glared at him for another minute then he looked away. He went closer to the front wheelhouse window and studied the sky. To Wally, who was watching him closely, and wondering at the same time if he could make a run for the door, the captain appeared to be looking into the sky for—something. Then he seemed to notice Wally as though for the first time.

'Get out!' He shouted.

Wally wasted no time in moving to the door, once through it, he ran as fast as he could along the deck to join up with the others. They had no idea what the captain might have done but releasing his wheelhouse captive surprised them. Once Wally was with them, Tommy motioned everyone to back up. They moved further away toward the bow and as far as possible away from the wheelhouse.

Quigley stood in the same place as he was before Sulkar's attack. Since he had made no overt move on them Tommy was led to believe that he was either too bewildered by what had happened to do anything—or he was on their side—or was neutral. In any event, it seemed, he posed no threat to them for the moment.

Then they heard the sound. The sound was like no other, not like the one that they had heard on those other occasions no, this was completely dissimilar. Perhaps it was the same instrument but the sound was different, it was louder and it had a frightening effect on them. An outlandish herald, a shrieking, piercing, prolonged wail. Some of them put hands over their ears in protection from the blast that seemed like it was about to tear into their brain. In fact it drove them further away, along toward the fore deck—away from the sound. But where, they wondered, was it coming from? Nowhere that they could say for certain. It seemed to come from nowhere and yet at the same time, from everywhere—to be everywhere. They looked to the wheelhouse but spray on the windows shrouded them from what the captain might be doing inside.

Quite suddenly, the sound stopped and a second after that the captain threw the front window open and stared in their direction. No one seemed able to stir, as though held in the grip by the terrifying eyes. The sound had stopped so abruptly that that in itself was chilling. If it could have been described as musical, it had stopped unnaturally in mid note. It seemed like it would go on forever now it was gone. Replaced with a silence so intense that the silence itself had a force if it's own. The wind stilled to nothing, there was a vacuity, a nothingness that was even more fear-provoking than the sound that had preceded it. Captain Burke turned his head away from them, to the sea.

'Look!' He pointed his outstretched arm through the open window, to the South. 'Look you!' he shouted, 'look you there!'

Tommy turned to the where he was pointing. For a moment he could see nothing. Then it appeared. He could see it moving toward them from the South. A huge, black mass of cloud was forming. An enormous dark shadow that covered, when he first saw it, only part of the sky then quickly, half of the sky. It rose up to an incredible height. In magnitude it rose from the sea to the sky—and was broadening quickly across from east to west and was to, in moments, stretch from horizon to horizon. Broiling and tossing the black mass was moving on them at a great speed. Flashes of lightning could be seem deep inside the cloud as it came on. Then they heard thunder, still a distance away but getting closer all the time.

The *Erehwon* steadied for a moment at first as though bracing herself for the onslaught that was to come. Then the ship began to pitch and roll. Though bloodied eyes the captain watched the black mass that was approaching with both dread and enchantment, a paradox in terror and elation. The blood flowed down into both of his eyes, which even so, appeared as though to be afire with a horrific glow.

Seconds later the storm hit the *Erehwon* port beam on with the force of a full blown hurricane. She almost rolled over with the first assault and those that could not grab hold of something were quickly thrown to the railings as she heeled to starboard. Tommy and Val and all of the others were hurled across the deck. The captain turned the bow into the wind and the ship began to right herself from the rolling motion and instead began an ever deepening pitch forward. Then the bow lifted high into the air only to descend again deeper into the water and higher into the air with each pitch forward.

'We shall see who of you is worth your salt,' Captain Burke shouted, 'we shall see who can battle the sea!'

The *Erehwon* was now facing the full onslaught of the fiercest of storms. Beginning at the bow the ship took onboard giant waves that broke over the fore deck and ran the length of the ship. One after another huge mountains of water struck with pestilential ferocity, each wave bigger and more powerful than the one before. The captain welcomed the great waves as they were hurled up to his window.

'Quigley!' he shouted, 'set them to work! Man the halyards, reef in! reef in!' He spun the wheel hard over to port then seconds later, back the other way to starboard causing the ship to corkscrew. 'We'll soon know who is fit to serve the mighty ocean!'

Tommy turned to the man standing with them who now seemed so small. The man who was no longer the formidable first mate of those early days on the ship. Now he was as insignificant and helpless as the rest of them. Holding on and staring at the wheel house just as they were, just as uncertain of what to do. Tommy figured, he was all they had.

'Mister Quigley!' He yelled over the raging wind.

There was no answer.

'What'll we do?' he shouted, 'Quigley! What should we do?'

Quigley did not seem to hear over the noise of the storm or if he had heard it did not seem to register. Tommy turned to help Val who was having trouble holding onto the railing. She also pleaded with the now seemingly immobilized first mate.

'Mister Quigley!' Val yelled.

With sea water and pelting rain crashing into her face she was about to lose her grip on the railings and would surely have been thrown into the sea if Tommy had not grabbed her and held on. He shouted something but the wind took his words. Others were screaming too, some hysterically. Others cried out for help trying to lift their voices over the raging wind.

'Quigley! Mister Quigley!' Tommy shouted into his face. Quigley seemed to be in a trance, staring blankly. Tommy grabbed him by the shoulders and shook him.

'Help us! You son of a bitch, help us! What can we do?'

'What?'

'What are the orders!' Tommy shouted back to him. 'Mister Quigley! Tell us what we should do!'

If they thought that they had experienced the storm's peak, they were wrong, for now the full force of the storm hit the ship. Huge waves heeled the *Erehwon* over to a point where she was about to have breached but the captain's maneuvering from the wheelhouse saved her time and again. Gigantic waves dashed across the deck, at times engulfing the entire vessel from stem to stern and beam to beam. Tommy knew they had to steady the ship through the storm but only the first mate could tell them what to do.

'Quigley!' Tommy shouted. 'Do something!'

Out of the stupor that had held him immobilized Quigley suddenly came to his senses.

'Do as the captain says, he's at the helm, he is the only one who can save the ship! Quigley shouted back but they could barley hear his words over the screaming noise of the storm. 'Haul down on the sheets!' He called, 'take in all but that mainsail,' he pointed, 'we have to have sail to make way, something that he can to steer her by!'

That was all they needed to propel them into action. They started to haul in the sails and everything else that Quigley ordered them to do without thinking about it except perhaps to be grateful for the intense training of those early days on the ship. They seemed to act almost as one in running to the sheets that he had indicated and Quigley himself was now hauling on. It was no easy task, first of all they had to keep from being flung into the sea and at the same time haul down the sails and the other things that Quigley was ordering them to do. Tommy and Val, with the others worked furiously to save the ship while at the same time holding on for dear life to whatever was at hand, a railing, a mast, an outcropping of superstructure, something, anything.

The storm exhilarated Captain Burke. Alternatively calling out orders that might save the ship and crying up to the heavens to send their worst down to destroy it—and at the same time, calling orders.

'You there, secure that line! Aloft! Up you go! Secure that sheet! Now we'll see what you're made of!' He yelled at Quigley and the others then looked upwards to the sky. 'Bring me your mighty burst,' he cried, 'for I am ready!'

But Quigley shook his head, it was unnecessary, no one was going to try to climb into the rigging. 'No!' he cried, 'you can't go up there—just cut the lines, let the sails go to the wind!'

They took to the knives and began to cut away at the ropes and lines releasing the sails to fly off instantly. Stripping the ship as though she were a distressed, dying animal and that the canvas on her a shroud. The captain had, at this point, it seemed to Quigley and those like Tommy who were able to take a quick look at him in those minutes, had crossed over into madness. His face contorted into an ugliness that filled those who could see him during flashes of lightning, with chilling terror. Blood ran freely down his face filling his crazed eyes, making him a grotesque sight to behold. At those times when the lightning was not flashing they were encased in a terrifying blackness.

'Quigley!' the captain shouted, 'the main topsail peak halyard, look man! She's going, get a man up there, and there, the mizzen royal stay!' He ordered uselessly, none of them were going to obey the orders of a madman, they used their knives instead.

'Stand by lee braces!' he yelled.

No one could make it even half way up the rope ladders of the mast and survive, Quigley shouted at them. 'Just do what he says down here on deck! Use your knives cut away all the ropes and lines!'

'Do it!' Tommy working furiously at what Quigley was telling them to do, called to those that could hear him, 'cut them—cut them all!'

He was hacking at the nearest ropes with Val by his side. Soaked with sea water as they were made the thick, heavy ropes almost impossible to cut through.

Captain Burke spun again the wheel causing the *Erehwon* to heel over violently, pitching and rolling in every direction not only because of the storm but the captain's maneuvers—spinning the wheel first to the left then right—yet, because of what he was doing and in some instances, in spite of what he was doing, the *Erehwon* stayed awash but afloat.

Sulkar, after the attack on the captain, had staggered away to the forward part of the middle deck, there he had collapsed. The water coming over the deck washed him up against one of the railings near the wheelhouse where he stumbled around trying to get to his feet. With a great effort he was able to move along a few feet against the weight of the water at that point he came into the captain's view. Upon seeing Sulkar, the captain turned the wheel fast to starboard then he stared for a moment upwards, into the rigging. The ship dipped violently. One of the spars broke away from the masthead and came crashing to the deck bringing all the attached lines and ropes with it. The rigging lines and ropes quickly became entangled with the weak Sulkar. Some of the lines wrapped around his body but one rope slipped higher, to his neck and encircled it.

Captain Burke turned the wheel to port sharply and the rope around Sulkar's neck became taught. A wave hit the side of the ship and heeled her over so as to cause another spar snap and fall to the deck on the forward side of the mast taking the rope with it. Sulkar was at first dragged along the deck then quickly hauled up to ultimately hang from the highest yardarm on the ship. For a few minutes, he struggled hopelessly to get free. There was to be no escape, he was slowly being strangled to death. Finally, Sulkar's arms fell limp to his side and he swayed back and forth with the motion of the ship, the eye, that single freakish orb bulging out of his twitching head. The captain acknowledged Sulkar's execution with a nod. Gratified in the knowledge that the appropriate sentence had been carried out. Hanging from the yardarm was the fitting punishment for mutineers.

The captain wasted no more time on the hanging man instead he turned his attention to someone else who had fallen within his field of vision. Karen was pitched away from the rest of them by one of the waves and she was now struggling to get herself back to the outstretched hands of the others. The wheel turned again so as to make the ship fall off and roll in another direction. With this action Karen was thrown off her feet and began, with ever increasing speed, a long slide that sent her sprawling along the entire length of the deck. As the ship came up at the stern Karen left the deck and was hurled out into midair. For Karen all sound was eradicated save for the rush of air that entered her ears. Her face horror stricken, she screamed. But there was no sound from the scream. Her body continued its flight in soundless air until it hit the water with terrible force and disappeared quickly beneath the surface. With the impact of her body on the water the noise of the storm's fury was restored. But Karen would hear nothing more as she was carried deeper beneath the surface of the whirling sea.

Twenty

Quigley struggled along the bucking deck back to a place near the wheelhouse. With most of the lines and ropes now cut away several of the others felt that they could do nothing but hold on. Some of them huddled together in groups jamming themselves between the superstructures and the railings hoping that if they held onto something, even each other, they would not be washed overboard into the sea.

But Tommy and Val along with Spencer and Jeff and some of the others were still fighting to save the ship knowing that the survival of the *Erehwon* would be their survival. They were knocked down time and again but at least for now, managed to hold on and at the same time chop away at the last of the ropes holding the sails.

To add to everything that was going on with the tempest and the struggle to save themselves, *Saint Elmo's fire* lightning, at that moment, struck the Erehwon. With nowhere for the electricity to escape, the entire vessel was lit up in the darkness in which the ship was totally engulfed. Spars and masts glowed fiercely with a weird bluish white light as though the whole ship were afire. The lighting of the ship was accompanied by loud crackling, it sounded as though thousands upon thousands of bone dry tree branches were burning fiercely.

The storm, with all its ferocity, had rallied Quigley from his stupor and he had been the driving force in saving the Erehwon. Certainly not by doing as the captain had ordered but more so perhaps by long years at sea and of course, a seaman's instinct. Now with most of the canvas cut away off her, she was able to ride the blast a little easier. Then, the captain turned her into the wind again and shouted again to Quigley.

'Mister Quigley! Come here!'

Tommy could see the captain calling orders to Quigley but he couldn't hear what the orders were because of the howling wind. The *Saint Elm O's Fire* gradually dissipated and the ship was plunged into a ghastly half-blackness. The captain barked more orders and threw something to him but Quigley just stood there not responding.

'Mister, you will obey me!'

Quigley stood directly in front of the wheelhouse window and did not move. He gave no sign that he was about to do whatever the captain had told him.

'Mister Quigley, do your duty!'

Quigley stood as still as the tumbling deck would allow. Infuriated at his disobedience, Captain Burke pointed the gun at him.

'You have five seconds to carry out my order!'

Quigley did not move.

The captain fired a shot from the revolver. The bullet smashed into Quigley's chest just below the breast bone. He staggered backwards but recovered quickly to once more stand defiantly before the captain.

'Do your duty, damn you! Damn you!'

The captain fired again—the bullets slamming into Quigley's neck and chest. They watched in horror as another shot put Quigley to the deck. He began to crawl toward them, then he was able to stand and stumble forward and disappeared down the forward hatchway.

The storm raged on unabated. Most of the crew were certain that they could not hold on much longer—that inevitably they were all going to be thrown into the sea. They had seen Karen hurled to her death and now they knew that to hold on as long as they could was the only natural response but many were beginning to feel it was hopeless. Everyone would die and they would die soon. And then, as though to confirm their fears, the killing began in earnest. Jim was swept along the deck unable to keep his feet under him, and became impaled on a boat hook that struck him in the back and came out in the center of his chest impaling him. His body sagged—and life drained from him.

The ship turned sharply again and a boom fell instantly crushing the life out of Patty. But the killing had only begun. A spar was washed over the side with lines dangling from it. Wally became tangled in the ropes and was quickly dragged to the railing. Unable to free himself, he begged for help. It all seemed to be happening at the same time. Those that were near him gave up their life lines and struggled through the water to come to his aid. At such a time human instinct, the will for individual survival, would surely have to take precedence over everything else in the human spirit. The dominating thought in each mind would be to save oneself. But that was not so, they were trying to help each other. The ropes around Wally became taut as the force of the water tugged the spar further away. He was pulled up and over the railing into the sea. Those that were trying to free him could, in the end, only watch helplessly as he was dragged over the side. His hand reached out to them as he was being taken away from the ship. They did not see Wally disappear beneath the waves. He simply drifted out of sight. His calls, even though most of them could not hear it after he was taken a few feet away, finally became stifled until there was nothing. Tony was washed over the side but managed to hang on to the upper part of the rail. Laura was close enough to help him. She gripped Tony around the arm and shoulder pulling him in until he was back on the shipboard side of the railing. A second later another mountainous wave engulfed them both. When the water washed away only Tony was there. Laura had been taken. He searched frantically over the side but there was no sign of her. Tony slumped down into the scupper well—gave up—and began to weep.

Below deck, Quigley wrestled with a stubborn hatch that was well forward of the main cabin. Finally he was able to pull it open and in so doing, sent himself tumbling to the deck. Then, crawling the rest of the way, he dropped down through another deck hatch into the bilge.

Tommy made his way over to where Tony lay huddled near the railing.

'Tony!' he yelled, 'Tony! You and the others try to free the long boat.'

Tony looked up at him blankly.

'Laura's gone.' He said.

Tommy pulled him to his feet roughly and shouted.

'Tony, get to the longboat—now!'

Tony nodded and started to make his way toward where the longboat was positioned on the midship superstructure.

'Spencer!' Tommy shouted, 'Spencer! You and Val come with me, we'll try to get food from below, Jeff, you come too.'

'Are you going to try to launch the long boat?' Spencer cried.

Jeff called out. 'It won't work, the boat will be swamped as soon as we get it in the water!'

'It might at that,' Tommy tried raising his voice above the noise of the wind and the water that was whooshing along all the decks, 'but that's how we're getting out of this! Get going Jeff!'

'It's our only chance!' Spencer yelled.

Quigley's strength was failing fast. He labored to turn the wheel of the sea-cocks. Once he got the wheel to turn a fraction, he had to rest before going on to turn it another half inch or so. Blood was running from his mouth, the bullets that had torn into his vitals from the captain's revolver had done their work. A trickle of water appeared. Slowly it grew to a stream and finally, a gush of green sea water began to fountain up through the sea cocks and on into the bilge. Quigley climbed the ladder leading up to the main cabin deck. He dragged himself through the doorway into the mess—there he collapsed.

Tommy, Spencer and right behind them, Val and Jeff made their way across the bucking deck. They made it to the aft companionway and down the steps into the main cabin. They could see Quigley and stopped for a second but Tommy urged them on pointing to the galley and pantry.

'Go on, get all the food you can lay your hands on, hurry!'

Water began to surge through from the bilge and onto the main deck and was now slowly creeping through the door into the mess cabin near where Quigley was laying.

Quigley cried out weakly.

'Come here boy!'

Tommy hesitated.

'Go ahead, get as much as you can,' he called to those in the galley, 'and get water too!'

'The long boat has water.' Jeff answered, he was already filling a sack, Val and Spencer were doing the same.

Tommy went to the other end of the cabin and knelt beside the first mate. Quigley seized Tommy's shirt with one hand. He tried to say something. Tommy struggled to get free from what he knew was a death grip—Quigley was soon to be a dead man. Tommy was finally able to release himself from Quigley's grip and looked down to see that Quigley had placed a key into his hand.

In the galley Val called to Spencer. 'That's enough, that's all we can carry, Spencer let's go!'

Jeff had already hefted two full sacks over his shoulder and was already on the move toward the stairs leading to the deck.

'Let's get out of here!' He yelled.

'Tommy!' Val called.

No answer.

She called louder, 'Tommy, we're done, let's go—Tommy!'

'Okay,' Tommy replied without turning, 'go on up!'

Water began to lap around Tommy's shoes, he looked through the doorway and past to the forward bulkhead. Now he could see water bubbling up through the hatch from the bilge below. It was already knee deep taking the forward part of the ship lower. Clearly the ship was going to founder.

Tommy lifted the first mate's head up out of the water that was rising fast. Quigley was trying to say something.

'Captain's . . .'

His eyes gaped at Tommy but saw nothing—Quigley was dead.

Tommy was lowering the body down into the water as the others hurried from the galley. They dashed through the main cabin to find Tommy still beside Quigley—water rising steadily around him—Jeff could now see a steady flow coming on through the forward companionway.

'She's sinking!' he shouted, 'we've got to get the hell out of here, she's sinking!'

He raced up the steps of the aft companionway with the other two ready to go up behind him as soon as Tommy joined them. But Tommy hesitated.

'Tommy, come on she's sinking!' Val called to him her hand already on the banister.

'Go on up, Val, I'll be along in a in minute.'

'There are no minutes left, Tommy!' Val cried, frantically.

'I just have to—'

'No, Tommy, you have to come up now!'

Tommy ran to her and urged her toward the steps.

'Go! I'll be along!' he told her as he shoved Val onto the steps. She went on up to the top of the stairway and stopped. Jeff was there already and urged her forward ahead of him toward the other side of the deck where the others were trying to get the long boat up on the divots and over the side of the ship.

Tommy took a another quick look at the rising torrent. He turned to Spencer.

'You too Spencer, Tommy said, 'go on up!'

'No, we get out together !' Spencer protested.

'I have to do something.'

'There's no time!'

Tommy opened his hand—the key.

'The captain's cabin,' he said.

Spencer looked at the key and shook his head.

'Spencer, I have to know.'

Spencer hesitated for only a moment.

'Okay, let's do it!'

They tore through the main cabin to the aft companionway to the door that had been locked ever since they had been on the ship. Tommy placed the key in the lock and turned it. The door opened to reveal another companionway at the end of which there was another door. The captain's cabin. Tommy wasted no time, he put the same key into the lock. Water was now beginning to build in the main cabin and the angle of the deck was becoming progressively, bow down. There was no time to waste. The door swung inward.

The storm raged. As she came up on deck, Val could see that Tony and the others had been able to get the lashings and cover off the longboat. Although handicapped by the violent lurching of the ship they were able to get the boat free of all the tie downs and ready to launch. But to send the long boat into the wild sea? It seemed that they would be leaving one hell to enter another. And the killing was not over. Frankie was washed over the side, his screams for help unheard by the others. A second later Helen was hurled along the deck, her body smashing viciously into the base of the wheel house taking the life from her instantly. Captain Burke seemed not to notice, even though her body had crashed with a bone shattering thud against the wooden structure. The captain had appeared to steer the *Erehwon* to the left and just as suddenly, right, and in a way that with almost every turn of the wheel another of the them was killed or thrown overboard. By now he was greatly weakened from the brutal wound and the ensuing loss of blood. His movements were becoming sluggish. From time to time his head would drop down and it was becoming a great effort for him to lift it again.

Tommy and Spencer stepped inside the captain's cabin. Sparse quarters indeed, a bunk, with drawers under it, on the other side of the cabin, a small bench and little else. Over by the aft bulkhead a curtain extending from the floor to the overhead and across from side to side across the width of the cabin. Tommy moved over to it. He found the cord that would draw the curtain and pulled it, revealing a large tank. The water inside was dull and hard to see though but they were able to make out that there was definitely something in it. As they went closer to the glass they could see two vague forms—the forms were moving—it was hard to see, the cloudy water made it difficult to make out anything clearly, but there was something.

Through the shadowy water they saw what appeared to be some kind of creatures. They could see that, whatever they were, had limbs. Limbs that seemed as though they were old, not old—perhaps—emaciated. Then, they saw something else looking up at the torso of the creatures, they saw that the forms had faces—faces that were indistinct and almost featureless. Nevertheless there was something about them that made them different from each other. Looking closer they could distinguish a vague expression on each. They moved closer. The horror bared on the faces of Tommy and Spencer could only be matched by the pitiful expressions of the creatures in the tank—which seemed to be alive. Then a shock that made them back up, however involuntary. Tommy and Spencer stared transfixed at the two objects in the glass tank and presently a terrifying realization hit them. And it hit both at the same moment.

'Oh, God no!'

'Beth and Alex.'

'Oh, it is them but . . .'

Spencer began to speak. He spoke as a scientist might perhaps speak after gathering his thoughts, clinically.

'Glorianna said, Tritons are of the deity, supreme beings, but of the lower order of the deity. That is to say bad, not good, and at the same time, of the origin of mind from the brain of the supreme being and that they are neither male or female, but a single and independent power.' Spencer paused as they stared at their friends who were not their friends any more but something else. 'She said Tritons cannot make offspring in the normal way.'

There was that expression on what were once the faces of Beth and Alex. But they were not Beth and Alex any more, they were something else. Were they alive? They were moving. They looked as though they were dead but in some way they appeared as though they were not dead—they could not be dead—they were moving.

'Sulkar hit the captain with an axe.' Tommy murmured.

'Yes, an axe,' Spencer exclaimed 'Glorianna said that Tritons can only be killed with an axe.'

'An axe.' Tommy, almost inaudible his voice dull as though he had not heard Spencer. But he had and Tommy made up his mind. He left the cabin quickly and went through to the companionway. The main cabin deck was now had more than two feet of water swilling around. It was hard to move through but Tommy made his way purposely. He ripped a large ship's fire axe from the bulkhead. He went back to the captain's cabin as fast as the water would allow.

Spencer watched Tommy but didn't say anything. Tommy hesitated for only the briefest second then swung the axe hard. The glass shattered instantly, spilling water and the two miserable occupants out onto the cabin floor in a torrent. A profound change came over Tommy at that moment. Spencer realized what Tommy intended to do.

'Don't Tommy! Don't do it!

Tommy took a firm grip on the axe handle and lifted it in the air.

Those on deck were about to lower long boat into the raging water.

'I'm going back.' Val said pulling Jeff closer so that he could hear what she was trying to tell him.

Jeff grabbed her by the arm.

'You can't go back down there!'

'I'm going below,' Val yelled at him.

'You can't!' Jeff took her arm in a stronger grip and held on tight, 'look she's going down! The bow is almost under already!'

'Let me go!' Val struggled to get free.

The axe rose high.

'No' Spencer cried, 'No!'

Tommy bought the axe down with great force. He took a step and raised the axe and smashed it down a second time—he stood back and stared down.

Twenty One

Captain Burke lifted his head, his eyes closed tightly for a moment, then when they opened, a desperate look of anguish began to cover his face. It was as though a knife had, at that very moment, been driven into his heart. Bloodied and horrifying though the countenance was, the stern features needed strength to be maintained, now with that strength collapsing, the features softened.

Tony, with the help of Sui Ming and Matthew, had been successful in launching the longboat and now it was lashed to the side of the ship. Jeff and Val had bought the food rations up on deck and now Matthew handed the bundles down to Mary and Jenny who were already in the boat. Glorianna had made a place for herself near the bow and was now huddled down between two of the benches, almost invisible. As well as the lashings, the others were holding the long boat close to the ship with ropes around the bollards.

Tommy stood looking down. Then he stood back and threw the axe against the far bulkhead. Spencer had to drag him out of the cabin. As he did so Spencer took a moment to notice the captain's malodorous and frugal rations. Could that be the origin of the smells that had disturbed them so much he wondered.

The water was chest high as they made their way to the companionway steps leading to the deck. Spencer climbed several rungs of the stairway but Tommy paused to take one last glance around the main cabin.

'Come on! Tommy! Come on!'

'Yeah, okay.'

Spencer started up the stairs. Tommy grabbed the railing to pull himself out of the water and onto the stairs when something obstructed his movement. Quigley's body floated between him and the lower companionway. The eyes, still open wide, stared sightlessly up at him. Jolted, but considering the events of the last minutes it meant very little, he simply pushed the body away. It drifted further into the main cabin, bobbing up and down listlessly with the motion of the water, so unlike the frenetic quickness of the erratic first mate in life. Tommy turned just as a large piece of the overhead snapped off and came crashing down on his neck and shoulder. He was not completely knocked out but stunned enough to make him fall. Tommy, laying down there on the lower steps leading to the deck and safety—tried to take hold of the railing again but his hand splashed uselessly inches away from it. Again, he reached out desperately but couldn't make it. One final effort and he had a grip on the railing but he wasn't able to gather enough strength to pull himself up—he let go of the railing—Tommy's eyes closed.

Val was the only one, of those on deck, that was not in the longboat. She had yanked herself away from Jeff who had in turn been shoved into the boat by some of the others. She ran to the top of the companionway and stopped dead. She tried to think about what she was doing. It took less than a second for her to come to a decision. If Tommy was not coming up she would go down to where he was. Val stepped inside the companionway that led to the steps going down to the main cabin. Spencer, running the other way up the staircase careered into her. Tommy was nowhere in sight.

'Where's Tommy?' Val shouted at him, 'where is he?

'He's coming, he's right behind me.'

'Okay, take off—get to the boat!'

She pushed past Spencer and went on down the companionway. She had taken only a few steps down before she could see that the cabin was flooding quickly. Tommy was there on the lower rungs of the staircase. She could see that he was not making any effort to climb the stairs. He had been stunned into immobility, in the grip of an inertia that would not allow him to move—even to save his life. Water was lapping around his chest and rising fast—in another minute Tommy would go under completely. Val wasted no time. She grabbed him by the shirt and with a huge effort hauled him out of the water and got him to his feet. He was upright and beginning to move with her but fell backward—taking Val with him—into deeper water—both of them went under. Val was able to reach a hand out and grab the staircase railing—the other hand held fast to Tommy's shirt. Val was able to get herself to the surface dragging Tommy behind her. Now she had to fight the water and at the same time pull Tommy along behind her. Finally she was able to get them both to the steps again.

There was no time, the water was coming faster now, rising higher by the second. Pushing him in front of her, they began to climb the steps, slowly one step then the next. Val pushed him ahead of her for another two steps then moved ahead again to go in front for a better purchase and began pulling him up the stairs.

She was using every once of her strength but it wasn't enough, Tommy was heavy and laden with the weight of the water. The same water was increasingly trying to pull them back and was now more than keeping pace with their struggle up the stairs—it was rising on them faster than their progress up the stairs—chest high and rising fast. Twice Tommy's head went under water. Although discarded almost instantly, the thought occurred to Val that she could not get him out before the cabin was totally flooded. As hard as she pulled him the water was dragging them both back into the cabin. Gathering a combination of strength of mind and whatever power was left in her body Val determined she would not let him drown.

'Tommy! Snap out of it!' She shouted.

Then, with one hand still hauling him up the stairs with the other she unleashed a mighty slap to his face. Slowly, Tommy began to come out of the torpor and started to move with her. Still the water was rising faster than they were climbing. With one last supreme effort and by crawling the last steps they were suddenly at the top and standing on deck. She took his hand in hers and began to move faster to the side of the ship and the long boat. Tommy, even though now more aware of where he was and what was happening, still allowed her to lead him as they ran.

Spencer was already climbing down into the long boat when Val and Tommy reached the side of the ship. They were about to step down into the boat but suddenly he shoved Val ahead of him. The deck in front of them was awash now. The ship was settling by the bow. The stern began to lift making her ready to take the final plunge into the depths. Tommy looked back to the wheelhouse.

Captain Burke stared at him. The captain seemed to know everything that had happened on the deck below. An expression of profound sadness had fallen upon him. He knew also that his ship was going to the bottom. There was no fear only the expression of despondency that became fixed on his bloodied, face. The long boat lay lower in the water than the ships deck so no one else could see the wheelhouse. Tommy alone was still on the deck and only he could see the captain. The squall even though dying now could still be heard—but the terrifying storm furor was being replaced by different sound—the lingering, placid note of wind passing through the rigging. The captain then leaned forward and outside of the wheelhouse window.

'North by north east, boy,' he called, north by north east.'

Tommy looked at him for a long moment and finally nodded.

'North by north east it is . . . captain.'

As the last of the gentle note of the wind through the rigging died, so died the storm. As suddenly as it had started, the fearful barrage of wind and water began to abate. And then to be gone. Not to move off to some other place in the ocean, no, the great storm that had appeared from nowhere now dissolved into nothing. Straightaway the wind quieted to little more than a soft zephyr and the sea calmed to stillness. The captain lifted his bloodied head once more. This time the call was stronger leaving no doubt as to who was still master of the *Erehwon*.

'Abandon ship!' Captain Burke issued his last order.

'All hands . . . abandon ship!'

Tommy climbed down into the longboat and they pulled away from the dying ship and it's dying captain. They didn't have to row, the longboat just drifted away from the ship in a docile manner without any help. The sea pacified now—the horror of before was gone. A hushed, spiritless pall descended on them as they stood off and watched the last of the ship. It occurred to many of them that they should hate her and indeed, that they did, at first. But looking at her now, in her final minutes of her life, it seemed that she bore a vast dignity about her, a patrician splendor. Something that told them it was not the ship that had carried out the destruction of their friends, their shipmates. It was not the ship. It was someone, something, else. Not the ship. Not their ship.

The bow went down slowly making hardly a ripple in the smoothing water. The upper fore deck followed soon after. Spencer placed a hand on Jeff's shoulder. Jeff swallowed hard as he watched the 'Larrikin's deck' go under. The brass plate was going to lay on the bottom of the ocean forever. Jeff did not look to see whose hand it was, it didn't matter who it was, they all felt something.

Next to surrender, the fore works where the first mate and bos'n quarters were. Recent memories flooded back to them. The ship was not angled up so much at the stern now. It seemed as though she had found the most submissive incline in which to make her descent. Water began to gather in languid eddies around the wheelhouse. Still holding the helm, Captain Burke, eyes ever forward he and only he, could be the one to guide his ship to the bottom. The water climbed to the window and spilled over the sill swamping the wheelhouse. The captain held fast to the helm as the sea engulfed him. Captain Burke disappeared from sight.

Strangely, the stern rose ever so slightly for a moment and then settled back, perhaps in a final salute before slipping silently below the surface. The masts and yards followed quickly. The water swirled briefly. Moments later there was nothing to say that a proud ship had been there.

The last voyage of the *Erehwon* had ended.

Twenty Two

Five days after casting off from the *Erehwon*, land was in sight. The sail filled from a fair wind out of the south west encouraging the sturdy longboat to cut along at an eager pace. Tommy was at the tiller with Val by his side. To the east, between them and the horizon, a large cargo ship could be seen by everyone in the boat. Spencer took Val's place when she left to sit beside Mary and one of the other girls for a while. Spencer waited a little before speaking.

'How far do you think we've sailed?'

'I don't know.' Tommy answered absently, his thoughts elsewhere. 'I should have made sure.'

'You didn't have to, they were already dead.'

'But what if they weren't, they would want me to kill them wouldn't they? Jesus! What did he do to them?'

'The sea is a mysterious place.' Spencer answered vaguely.

'I wish I knew if they were really dead.'

'They were dead.'

'Listen,' Tommy said, 'let me ask you to just suppose for a moment?'

'Okay.'

'Suppose they weren't dead.'

'But —'

216

'Just for a moment, not dead, and let's say that they really were Tritons—'

'That's a lot of supposing.'

'Yes, but if they were, then they might still be alive and if so, they'd be able to get out of the wreck, wouldn't they?'

'Yes, I guess so, but they *were* dead—dead Tommy, dead. Their bodies were already decomposing,—what we saw was them being moved around by the motion of the water and that made them look as though they were alive . . . and, they had probably been dead ever since they went missing.'

They were silent for a few minutes before Tommy spoke again.

'What about the storm? Did he make the storm happen?'

'No!' Spencer declared emphatically. 'He knew the weather and how to read it. Maybe he thought he could control the weather but nobody can do that.'

'How do you explain everything else that happened?'

'Logically.' Spencer paused for a moment before going on. 'Logically—for most of what happened. But it was my mistake to consider some theories. Grasping at ideas that were bought about by fear and suspicion.'

'You can't blame yourself for that.'

'I mean theories that were illogical, and I went along with some of the clues.'

'Made no difference in the end—he did kill them.'

'Yes, by maneuvering the ship and of course, Beth and Alex. The rest of it was—'

'Was . . . what?'

'As I said, the sea is a mysterious place, we've found that to be so. Most of the things that happened out here have a logical explanation some of it coincidence, then there are things, some things, that can't be explained.'

'A lot of things.'

They said nothing for a time then, still looking out over the vast sea, Spencer broke the silence.

'It's over.' He said.

Tommy gazed thoughtfully at the other survivors in the long boat.

'Yeah,' he said finally, 'you're right, Spencer. It is over.'

Spencer stayed with Tommy for a little while longer. Then he went forward to a place near the bow and gazed through the light mist—to the Islands in the distance. After a few minutes he took a notebook from his jacket pocket and began writing.

Val moved back to Tommy's side, resting her head on his shoulder and linking her arm in his. She knew his thoughts were back there with the others who hadn't made it.

'I know,' she said quietly and closed her eyes for a moment then looked up again, toward what lay ahead. 'I know, Tommy.' she said so softly that it was little more than a sigh, 'And yet we are—in love. In light of everything that's happened, do you think love seems irrelevant.'

'It's not irrelevant but—'

'Listen to me,' Val cut him off, 'maybe we shouldn't be alive either, but we are. Tommy, we're alive.'

He felt her closeness, closer than ever before.

Jeff pointed to the cargo ship, now only a few miles away.

'Shall we try to get them to pick us up?'

'No.' Tommy answered sharply.

Through the mist and in the distance, Mount Mona Vatu climbed out of the sea beckoning them. Vanua Levu Island could be seen vaguely as they approached the windward side of the Fijian Islands.

'No, Jeff, we'll make it on our own.'

Since casting off from the doomed *Erehwon* most of them had been engaged in sailing the long boat in one way or another and the shared mood had been somber. But land had been sighted shortly after dawn and spirits in the boat were picking up rapidly. There was more talking and the insouciant Jeff even cracked a joke that resulted in a smattering of laughter. Tommy and Val smiled when they heard Glorianna admit that it was she who had taken the batteries and thrown them over side. Mary was resolutely getting back to her persnickety self when she told the others, 'My father will be very disappointed—it was an excellent camera.'

She saw Jeff roll his eyes. 'He will!' Mary admonished.

Val sniffed back the wetness—wiped her eyes with the back of, first one hand, then the other—the little boat that was taking them to safety didn't run to tissues—and gathered her thoughts, landlubber—sailor or psychologist—life goes on.

She sniffed mightily again and smiled coquettishly up at him. 'You know Tommy,' she said smiling innocently, 'we never did have that discussion on what we plan to do about us staying together?'

He didn't have to think about it so answered quickly.

'Val, how about we postpone the discussion?

'Postpone or reschedule?'

'Okay—reschedule.'

'Is there going to be a date for this rescheduling?'

'Yes there is, I propose—'

'Propose?'

'Yes, I propose that we *do stay together*,' Tommy said with absolute sincerity and conviction, 'and reschedule that talk for exactly ten years from today, 'What do you say to that and ten years?'

'I say yes, adamantinely yes, but how about twenty years?'

'Thirty and you've got a deal?'

'Deal.'

They were quiet for a moment then Tommy smiled.

'Do you want to know something, Val?'

She nodded. 'Yes.'

'There was a test after all.'

The mist lifted. The Islands became clearly defined against a cloudless sky. Painted on the stern of the longboat, the name of the ship from which it came, *Erehwon*. The longboat, a little vessel that was no more than a speck on the great ocean was sailing smoothly to safe harbor.

THE END